PITCH

WILL PARKINSON

Harmony Ink

Published by
Harmony Ink Press
5032 Capital Circle SW
Ste 2, PMB# 279
Tallahassee, FL 32305-7886
USA
publisher@harmonyinkpress.com
http://harmonyinkpress.com

Cover Art by Reese Dante
http://www.reesedante.com

Cover content is being used for illustrative purposes only
and any person depicted on the cover is a model.

ISBN: 978-1-62798-034-0
Library ISBN: 978-1-62798-036-4
Digital ISBN: 978-1-62798-035-7

Printed in the United States of America
First Edition
August 2013

Library Edition
November 2013

I'M GOING to be honest, I never expected to be at this point. If it wasn't for some absolutely amazing people in my life, I would have never come to the point where my name would be on an actual book. It is these people I owe so much thanks for not allowing me to give up on my dream and making sure that I chased it until *Pitch* was born.

My mom—The dream had to start somewhere
Eden Winters—Muse and she to whom I owe so much
KC Wells—Friend, cohort, and keeper of secrets
Jo Peterson—aka Epic Sexy Goddess of the Universe
Tom Webb—He who is awesomeness personified
Laura Harner—She who is rock solid and rocks hard
Cate Ashwood—She who fell in love with my boys
Mardee Barnett—She who held my hand many nights
Grace Santiago—She who put a smile on my face
Mary Grzesik—She who called me bro and pushed me forward
Michelle Odden—She who said 'you can' and I did
Sean Ryan—He who cried manly tears
Lis Craig—She who urged me to move forward
Paul Parkinson—He who cooked while I wrote

I offer humble thanks to each of you. Without you, Taylor, Jackson, and my beloved Benny would never exist. And my dream would never have come true.

CHAPTER ONE
START AT THE BEGINNING

TAYLOR ANDREWS glanced toward the door and noticed a young man, shoulders hunched, waiting outside the classroom. As he continued to stare, the newcomer took a deep breath, threw back his shoulders, and lifted his head before he stepped into Mrs. Wagner's homeroom. He walked with purpose toward the front of the classroom and handed the teacher a sheet of paper without saying a word.

After a brief moment of studying the paper, Mrs. Wagner smiled at the young man before turning to the students filling the desks of her classroom. "Class, this is Jackson Kern. It's his first day here, and I need a volunteer to help him get acclimated."

Taylor looked at the new guy and felt his face heat. He grabbed his ever-present sketchpad from his backpack, his desire to capture this stranger's likeness overwhelming. The guy was... well, gorgeous. Taylor's hands flew over the paper as he took in Jackson Kern's beautiful well-sculpted face, rich chocolate-brown eyes, and dark, thick hair. He had a toned body, maybe a swimmer? God, what he wouldn't give to....

"I'll show him around, Mrs. Wagner," Becca Monroe offered brightly, interrupting Taylor's wayward thoughts.

"Thank you, Becca," Mrs. Wagner said with a smile before turning to the newest addition to the class. "Jackson, please take a seat. Becca will walk with you and show you the building and where your classes will be. If you have any questions, just ask her."

"Yes, ma'am, thank you," the new kid replied. Taylor noted how polite Jackson was, unlike most of the guys in his tenth-grade class.

Jackson parked his tall, lanky body in the seat next to Becca and started talking. Taylor watched as Becca's eyes roamed over Jackson's frame, and she licked her lips. He could tell she was already on the prowl. She was a pretty enough girl, if you liked them. Long reddish-brown hair, big green eyes, and a big... ego. She was hot and she knew it. She was also the kind of girl who was only out for one thing. Herself. She was junior varsity head cheerleader, something his best friend, Benny Peters, always had a lot of fun commenting on. She'd dated the captains of most of the sports teams, always switching to a new guy at the beginning of the season.

"Damn lucky girl," Taylor muttered. If he hadn't been enjoying the sight of the new boy, he'd have volunteered for guide duty. Oh, the things he wanted to show him... not that he had any experience; he'd never even kissed another boy. He worked hard at trying not to look at other guys. The thought of being outed in high school scared him, so much so that he'd sometimes have panic attacks when he thought about it—clammy skin, problems breathing, feeling faint. He hated those, really hated not being in control. It always made him feel weak and needy.

The bell rang, startling Taylor out of his reverie, and the students moved like cattle, heading off to their next class. Taylor scowled when he saw Becca take the new guy by the arm and lead him from the classroom. As they passed he heard Jackson ask, "Do you know who I talk to about the baseball team?"

"What position do you play, Jackson?" Becca asked excitedly, ignoring Jackson's question.

"I'm a pitcher."

Taylor could hear the excitement in Becca's voice, and he knew the reason. Baseball tryouts would be in the next week or two, and she needed a new ball-playing boyfriend since her ex, Cody Daniels, graduated. It was as if she'd won the freaking lottery. Jackson was hot *and* he played sports. For Becca that was definitely the best of both worlds.

2

Taylor chuckled. Oh, how he'd love to be that boy's catcher. But damn, Becca was probably going to be all over that anyway. Not that he'd ever have a shot with someone like Jackson. According to Benny, he wasn't bad-looking. Benny often said he was jealous of Taylor's curly blond hair, which he himself despised. *Besides*, Taylor thought, *Benny's straight. What does he know?* Jackson was probably three inches taller than Taylor's five foot eight, but it wasn't his height that bothered him as much as the extra weight. He was no one special, and someone like Jackson Kern would never give him the time of day. That's just how things went.

Over the next week, Taylor would see Jackson throughout the school. Other than homeroom they didn't have any classes together, but he noticed him in the hallway or heading to the gym. Taylor's heart fluttered every time he caught a glimpse of Jackson. He loved the way his lip curled when he was amused or the way he arched an eyebrow when he seemed to be curious about something. The thing that struck him most, though, was the fact that Jackson was so poised and confident when he was with a group. People hung on his every word. It almost seemed like he was holding court. People just tended to gravitate to Jackson. His rich baritone voice had a soothing, hypnotic effect on Taylor from a distance. He couldn't help but wonder what it did to the people Jackson was actually talking with. He watched Jackson in the school's weight room one afternoon and stood transfixed as the muscles in Jackson's chest and arms strained with every repetition. Taylor began to sweat and unconsciously licked his lips as he watched Jackson working his leg muscles. His pulse raced when Jackson pulled off his shirt, the dusting of dark hair across the expanse of his chest matted from sweat. Taylor swore he could smell Jackson's scent, musky but sweet. He wanted to get closer but knew it would seem weird, so he reluctantly tore himself away and went back to class.

Taylor was envious of Jackson's build. He studied his own body in the mirror and sighed. He was plump. That was the only way to describe it. There was no muscle definition. He tried to maintain his weight but couldn't resist pizza. He'd tried to work out with Benny, who seemed obsessed with his body, but it just wasn't for him. Taylor sighed heavily. He was so far out of Jackson Kern's league, he'd never have a shot with someone like him, but that didn't mean he couldn't enjoy the view.

TAYLOR glanced over at Benny, comfortably stretched out on the sofa, thumbing through Taylor's latest sketches. At six foot one and weighing in at nearly 215 pounds, Benny had always been one of Taylor's favorite sketch subjects. His eyes were the coolest brown color with small flecks of gold in them. His sandy hair was always cut short, but not like a buzz cut, which Taylor had to admit was his favorite kind of haircut.

Benny had always stood up for Taylor and it was that fact which made Benny the only one Taylor had come out to. No matter what else happened between the two, Taylor was sure Benny would always be there for him.

"Benny, what would you say if I told you I was crushing?" Taylor asked, sitting up on his bed and tossing a rolled-up pair of socks into the laundry basket.

Benny met Taylor's eyes as he laid the sketches across his chest. "I'd say who this time? Already over... what was his name? Mason? Dixon? Something southern."

"His name was Caleb," Taylor groaned, rolling his eyes. "And he was a jerk. Remember how he humiliated and made Toby cry when he came into the locker room and found Caleb throwing his clothes into the shower?"

"Yeah, I remember. I was the one who got him something to wear for the rest of the day. I can't stand bullies," Benny snarled. "So who has your undies in a bunch this time?

"I'm talking about the new guy, Jackson Kern. There's just something about him. He's... I dunno, different. He's not loud or annoying. He seems really laid-back. And he's totally hot. He just seems... perfect." Taylor sighed wistfully. "I can't imagine him ever doing a mean thing to anyone."

Benny tried to suppress a snort. "And how long is this one going to last? A month? Two tops. You go through crushes faster than I go through underwear."

"When you change them twice a year that's not too difficult," Taylor snickered.

Taylor was surprised when Benny hit him with a pillow, and the fight was on. He grabbed the other pillow and swung at Benny, who dodged and laughed. For such a big guy, Benny was surprisingly agile. They smacked each other around, laughing all the while, until Taylor cried uncle.

After they were exhausted, Benny turned to him and said with a sympathetic smile, "Taylor, talk to the guy. Pretty much the worst that could happen is he's not interested."

Taylor stared glumly up at the ceiling, his thoughts turning once more to Jackson. "No, the worst that could happen is he's a homophobic asshat who wants to kick the crap out of me."

"Yeah," Benny observed thoughtfully, "but at least he'd touch you. That's more than you've ever gotten before." He gave Taylor a gleeful grin, as if waiting for the comment to sink in fully.

And as soon as it did, Taylor lunged at Benny, and the fight was back on. Once Benny succeeded in pinning Taylor, his expression turned serious as he said, "Look, just be cool. Don't obsess. If you want to impress him, show him the pictures you drew of him. You're really good at doing these."

Taylor's cheeks heated. He could never show his work to Jackson. He didn't think they were good enough to share with anyone other than Benny. He'd been puttering around with drawing for years. He had several sketchpads full of various things that caught his eye. He loved to do drawings of nature scenes, people, and animals. He'd done several of Trip, his Siberian husky, before the poor dog died that still brought tears when Taylor looked at them. It was just a hobby, though. His father always told him he needed a real career and constantly reminded him that art wouldn't amount to anything in the real world. He shook his head sadly. No, there was no way Jackson would ever see his work.

STANDING by the bleachers near the dugout, Taylor couldn't help but wonder why he was there. Baseball tryouts held no interest for him. In fact, he'd always found the game kind of stupid, yet here he was. His gaze landed on Jackson Kern. Yeah, that was something he really wanted, to see Jackson play the game.

Jackson took the center thingy… the mound or whatever it's called. Taylor had spent a good deal of time reading about baseball. He figured he should know something about it, just in case Jackson ever spoke to him. Still, he was having a hard time wrapping his head around all the rules and terms. Didn't mean he wasn't going to try, though. He pulled out his sketchbook and did a few rough outlines, wanting to fill them out later. Jackson threw a few pitches to the catcher, loosening up. Mitch Daniels, Cody's younger brother, stepped up and tapped his bat on the ground. Jackson brought his arms up near his chest, struck a pose, and shook his head slightly. After a moment he leaned back and threw the ball. It went straight across the plate at blinding speed. Mitch swung at it and missed completely. When Jackson finished the inning, allowing no hits, he marched back to the dugout; the coach's jaw fell open as he rushed out to meet Jackson.

"Kid, what's your name?"

"Jackson, sir. My friends call me Jax."

"Well, Jax, if you can throw like that with consistency, you're gonna be our ace. I can tell," the coach said, practically drooling over the young prospect.

Taylor thought he saw Jackson… Jax blush. By the end of the tryouts, not one person had hit anything Jackson threw. When the coach told him he had a spot, Jackson smiled so big and wide, Taylor was sure his heart would stop. Then Becca came running over and threw her arms around the team's new pitcher. Taylor turned in disgust and started shuffling away, pausing to take a last look at Jackson. He was all hot and sweaty, and it looked really, *really* good on him. Taylor knew that's what he was going to be thinking about when he went to bed.

TAYLOR found himself drawn to watch the practices. He kept trying to tell himself it was stupid, and he knew it was, but he really enjoyed watching Jackson. He'd been going to watch practice every day for two weeks when he saw Jackson turn in his direction. For just a second he thought, more like hoped, that Jackson was looking at him. His eyes locked on Jackson, and his mouth went dry, wishing that he'd come over to him, put his arms around him, whisper in his ear... but then the guy turned and walked over to the rest of the team, clearing the field for the next inning. Taylor's heart sank, realizing it was all wishful thinking on his part.

"COME on, Taylor, crack a book. I came over to study, not to watch you stare at the ceiling," Benny huffed, pushing a pile of laundry off the chair and parking himself at the desk. "And would it kill you to clean up a little bit? This place is a sty, man."

Taylor never even registered the reproach in Benny's voice. All he could think about was Jackson.

"Benny, I'm going nuts. I know it's never gonna go anywhere, but I can't stop going to see him," Taylor groaned.

Benny stared at him, eyes wide. "Wow, never saw you this bad before. You'd always crush for a few weeks and then see some new hottie that made you forget the old one. Maybe you really do have it bad for this guy," Benny muttered.

Swinging his legs over, Taylor sat on the edge of the bed, grinning with excitement. "You've got no idea. Yesterday morning I saw him with a smear of toothpaste in the corner of his mouth. I swear it was one of the hottest things I'd ever seen, and I just wanted to lick it off."

Benny's lips tightened into a grimace. "Toothpaste is hot? God, you're so weird, Taylor. I hope you won't be upset if I don't admit to knowing you when we're in public."

Taylor smirked, remembering everything with vivid detail. "It was hot! If it wasn't for the fact that Becca rubbed it off for him, which really pissed me off, by the way, I'd have stared at it all day."

"So he and Becca are together?" Benny asked, putting the book down and finally turning to face Taylor.

"Yeah, I guess. She's always hanging on him and hugging him. It's totally disgusting," Taylor sneered.

"Because it's what you want to be doing?" Benny wondered aloud, keeping his voice low.

"Maybe." Taylor sighed. "Either way, this just reinforces my dislike of public displays of affection."

"So when are you gonna finally talk to him? How hard can it really be?" Benny asked patiently.

Taylor could see the look of pity on his friend's face, but he snapped, "Well, you get a girl to notice you and then come back and give me some pointers, okay?"

Taylor knew it wasn't fair. Benny was all about his schoolwork. His parents were always so strict about everything, and the schoolwork had to come first.

Benny quirked an eyebrow and stared at Taylor condescendingly. "I don't need a girl to notice me, Tay. I'm not the one who needs validation. Maybe *you* should just join the monks. I'm sure then you'll get plenty of hot action," Benny chuckled as he opened his math book. There was going to be a stupid quiz tomorrow, which, naturally, Benny was going to ace. He *always* aced them. Benny's grades were important to him. As it stood Benny had a near-perfect GPA and would likely be valedictorian as a senior.

He and Benny had been the best of friends since kindergarten. Taylor knew Benny would do almost anything for him, even if it included telling him things about himself he really didn't want to hear, especially when it was the truth. Taylor knew he was a chicken, but he also knew unrequited love would be better than being humiliated in front of or by Jackson.

CHAPTER TWO

'TIS THE SEASON

TAYLOR attended the first baseball game of the season. He'd never gone to any other sporting event at the school, but this was important. It would be Jackson's debut as the new pitcher, and Taylor decided he needed to be there to cheer him on. He knew it didn't make sense —his voice would be lost among all the others— but in his head it was a way he could show his support for Jackson. He'd tried to talk with him in homeroom. Jackson's smile made him seem approachable, but Becca wouldn't let Taylor get a word in. After a few minutes he just gave up and walked away. Tonight, though... tonight was all about Jackson. Taylor knew he'd shout and cheer for this guy. Win or lose, it didn't matter. It just mattered that he supported the pitcher.

Taylor's heart did a leap when Jackson marched out onto the field. Taylor could hear the crowd murmuring, talking about Jackson. A group of girls nearby were gushing about the young athlete, about how well he filled out the red-and-black jersey. Taylor felt a pang of jealousy when one of them mentioned Jackson's butt. He hated the fact that she was looking at it, even if it did look incredible. When Jackson reached the mound and turned to do his signature move, waving and bowing to the crowd, Taylor's chest swelled with pride, and he began cheering wildly for him.

The game was a total blowout. Jackson shut down the other side completely. It was a near-perfect game, except for one ball that got dropped by the second baseman. When the game was over, they'd won 12-0. Taylor wanted to rush out onto the field with everyone else, but Jackson was lost in the crush of people, getting his well-deserved accolades. Taylor trudged back home, jumped in the shower, and fantasized about Jackson Kern's performance.

The day after the game was a madhouse. Banners and flyers popped up overnight about the team and their star pitcher. Jackson had so many people around him, it was like he was a rock star or something. Taylor strode past and said, "Great game, congratulations," and continued on. He thought he'd heard Jackson say something, but he just kept walking. Throughout the day the buzz in school was all about Jackson. What he'd done. Where he'd been. How he and Becca were doing the nasty bump and grind—that part made Taylor nauseous. Even knowing that Jackson was bumping uglies with Becca, though, Taylor still wasn't able to get him out of his head. It was as if Jackson had crawled into Taylor's mind and taken up residence there. He'd begun noticing more of Jackson's mannerisms. How he'd touch the person he was talking to on the shoulder, hand, or sleeve. Nothing overt, but it seemed like he was trying to maintain a connection with the person. Taylor found it almost endearing.

TAYLOR sat down for lunch with Benny, the cafeteria food particularly unappetizing, and drummed his fingers, waiting for his friend to acknowledge him.

"Go ahead, Taylor, I know you've got something on your mind." Benny chuckled, not looking up.

Taylor gave a harsh sigh. "Benny, I'm going nuts. I tried to talk with him, but Becca was like a freaking pit bull. She seemed to be working extra hard to keep me away from him. Even if I was able to get near him, I think I'd probably just puke on him because I was so nervous."

"Charming picture." Benny grimaced, pushing away his lunch. "Thanks for the visuals. Let's say you did talk to him. If he wasn't interested in you as a boyfriend would you be cool just being his friend?"

10

Taylor's face scrunched up into what Benny called his thinking face for a few moments before replying.

"I don't think he needs a lot of those. He's got so many people hanging on him now, I doubt he'd have time for anyone else."

Benny snorted. "Oh please, those aren't friends, numbnuts. Those are fans. Those are the people who are your friends until something better comes along. If the season went to crap and Jackson was responsible, I guarantee you that none of those people, even Becca Monroe, would stand with him. That's the question. Would you?"

Taylor scowled. He couldn't believe Benny would even have to ask that question.

"Yeah, I don't really care about baseball, so it's not because he's famous," he mused, rubbing his chin. Then, much quieter, he added, "It's because he's... well... him. The package, not just the bits and pieces."

Benny laughed. "Leave it to you to make it about his package."

Taylor groaned but had to laugh. Benny always made him laugh at himself. After all, wasn't that what best friends did?

AFTER trying a couple of times to talk to Jackson in homeroom, Taylor pretty much gave up. Every time he got anywhere near, Becca would circle the wagons, and he wound up getting pushed away. He still ended up going to every practice and every game, though, always arriving early and staking out a spot close to the dugout where he could watch Jackson. The team was a powerhouse that season. They rolled over every other school, a perfect record in their fourteen games so far, tied for the best record in their conference. At this rate they'd be a shoo-in for state. Saturday's game was a tournament in Beloit. The team left early because it was a pretty far drive. Tournaments were not regular games and wouldn't impact their record, but the team really wanted the trophy. Taylor figured they'd need their stars to take the coveted award.

Taylor was late getting to the game because his stupid car wouldn't start. He begged Benny to give him a ride. It meant sneaking out, because no way would Benny's parents let him go to a baseball game when there was homework that needed an A. Benny grudgingly agreed to drive him, but told Taylor he owed him big time.

When they arrived it wasn't a pretty sight. The team was down by three runs in the sixth inning. Jackson seemed to be having control issues, something he'd never displayed until this point. His cool focus had vanished, and he paced and cursed to himself. Taylor pushed his way into the bleachers and near his usual spot, dragging Benny behind him.

Jackson ran out onto the field in the top of the seventh inning, closed his eyes, ran his fingers through his hair, and muttered something to himself before opening them and acknowledging the cheering crowd. His entire demeanor changed. He no longer looked anxious. He looked calm and determined. He slapped his cap on and approached the mound. He threw a flawless inning and the crowd went nuts. When the team came back onto the field, they scored a run, bringing them three away from winning the game. Taylor held his breath when Jackson came back onto the field. Benny put his hand on Taylor's shoulder as if to steady him. Jackson's first pitch was a little outside, but the next pitches were amazing. He again shut down the opposing team. As they prepared to switch for the inning, Jackson stood and gave a slight bow to the dugout. It was then that Taylor saw Becca, and his heart sank.

"Do you wanna go?" Benny whispered in his ear.

Taylor let out a heartfelt sigh. "No, I'm good. You asked me if I could be there as a friend, and I said yes. So if this is all I get, then I guess it will have to be enough," he replied, staring at Becca and Jackson in resignation.

"Aw, they're so cute when they grow up." Benny snickered.

Taylor elbowed him in the stomach.

The team won the tournament. Jackson's flawless late-game pitching got them out of a big jam, and the team rallied to score four runs in the ninth inning. There was a lot to celebrate. Becca was practically sitting in Jackson's lap, even before the team boarded the bus. Taylor went home with Benny, neither of them really saying much. Benny dropped Taylor off at his house before rushing off to do his homework. Taylor went to his room and changed. After puttering around the house for a while, he decided to start reading one of the new books he'd downloaded. He had several authors whose works he truly enjoyed and always bought their books when he could. His reading list for the week included *Fratboy and Toppy* by Anne Tenino, *Naked Tails* by Eden Winters, and a new one by SJD Peterson, *Tuck and Cover*. He lay down on the bed, Nook in hand, and started reading.

He jumped when the doorbell rang. He ran downstairs and looked out the window to see who it was. Jackson Kern was on his doorstep! His mind started buzzing. Why would Jackson be there? What could he possibly want? Taylor's palms began to sweat. He couldn't think of any reason Jackson was there. He heard the ringing before he realized he'd dialed Benny's number.

"Benny? Jax Kern is at my door!" Taylor whispered excitedly.

Benny sighed. "Sure, right. Look, I gotta finish my homework. Can I call you back?"

"No, seriously. Jackson Kern is standing at my door," Taylor huffed, carding his fingers through his hair.

There was a brief silence before Benny spoke. "Did you talk to him?"

"Why is he at my door?" Taylor asked aloud, not even registering Benny's question. There was a sigh of sheer exasperation from his friend.

"Taylor!" Benny snapped. "Why don't you just open it and ask him? Maybe they're doing candy bar sales for the team or something."

Taylor relaxed, breathing deeply, willing himself to calm down. "You're right. Hang on."

Taylor put the phone down on the table and opened the door just in time to see Jackson driving away. His heart sank.

"Well, fuck." He sighed heavily and picked the phone back up. "He drove away."

"Dude, you seriously blew it, and not in a good way. Monday morning ask him what he wanted. He was at your door, after all."

Taylor thought about it for a moment, realizing Benny was right. His panic faded. "You're right. I'll ask him when I see him at school."

"Now can I finish my homework? A 3.999 GPA isn't enough for my parents, and I need to find some extra credit work to do." Benny groaned.

After hanging up, Taylor realized he would spend the rest of the night wondering why Jackson had been at his door. He put away the Nook, deciding to lie down and think it over. Some of the scenarios he thought up were enough to make a Marine blush. Though he doubted they'd ever happen, even if Jackson could be that flexible

Sunday morning Taylor did not want to get out of bed. He'd stayed up too late, and his arm was sore. He felt his face warm and snickered a little thinking about the reasons. He rolled out of bed around noon and finished up his homework so he'd have the remainder of the day to himself. After a nice hot shower to relax his aching muscles, he called Benny and asked if he wanted to hang out for a while.

"You're only asking me to come over because you want to talk about Jax, right?" Benny asked knowingly.

Taylor tried to sound offended, but he knew it was true. He needed advice, and since Benny was the only person he was out to, that meant Benny needed to suck it up and deal.

"Please, Benny," Taylor whined.

"I just like hearing you beg." Benny cackled. "It makes me all tingly. I'll be over in twenty minutes."

Taylor grabbed a couple of Cokes and a bag of chips so he and Benny could snack while they talked. He figured if nothing else, Benny would be grateful for the effort.

Benny flopped his bulky frame onto the couch and grabbed a handful of chips, stuffing them into his mouth. "So let me get this straight, so to speak," he said, bits of chips spraying while he talked. "You drag me over here to listen to you go on about a straight dude that you're crushing on and being all weepy about, and all I get is some cruddy chips, which are stale, by the way."

Taylor took a deep breath. "Where do you want to go eat?"

"I'm thinking pizza would be good. Classic Slice in Bay View has some amazing choices."

Taylor smiled. He supposed he owed Benny that much. "Fine. Let me get my wallet."

Within a few minutes, they were out the door and headed for the restaurant. When they arrived they waited a few moments to be seated. The restaurant wasn't busy yet, which was a good thing since it was a small hole-in-the-wall place with just a few tables. Taylor sniffed appreciatively at the tantalizing aromas, and it started his mouth watering. He realized he was actually pretty hungry.

"Okay, a few ground rules," Benny said as they sat down. "First off, I don't want to know what you did after you saw him at your door. There is so much ick factor involved in that, I cannot begin to describe it. Second, we won't talk about how you two should be together. If you don't have the balls to talk with the man, then you obviously don't deserve him. Finally, I get to decide the pizza toppings. I know how much you like the meat—" Benny coughed. "—and I'm not going to comment further on that, but since I'm a vegan, we're getting one of their veggie cheese pizzas. I've heard they're awesome."

Taylor let out a frustrated huff. "So I have to pay for food *and* get lectured?"

"Yep. Take it or leave it." Benny's eyes danced with amusement. Taylor sighed and shrugged.

"Fine, but you're leaving the gratuity." Taylor pouted, slumping in his chair.

"Damn, I was hoping you were going to say tip. I had a whole joke set up for that one," Benny said with a mock scowl.

Taylor chuckled gleefully. "I figured, and that's exactly why I didn't say it."

"Okay, listen... I know you think you've got it bad for Jackson, but—"

Taylor cut off his words with a shake of his head. "I don't 'think' I have it bad, I know I do. It's nearly impossible for me to get through a day without seeing him or talking about him. I think about him all the time. Last night after he was at my door, I went upstairs to—"

Benny held up his hand, waving it frantically at Taylor. "Whoa, rule number one—I do *not* want to know what you did after you saw him at your door."

Taylor glared at his friend and then rolled his eyes. "Don't be an ass. I went upstairs to figure out what I should do the next time I see him. Is it rude to tell him I saw him at the door but was too busy picturing him naked to answer it? Or should I just be honest and say I was scared witless?" he asked, uncertainty evident as his voice cracked slightly.

Benny eyed Taylor sympathetically. "I don't think it matters what you say, as long as you actually say something. If he's at all interested in you, then you'll find out. If he's not, then maybe you can stop obsessing over him and find a real boyfriend."

Taylor scrunched his face up.

Benny tossed his napkin on the table, muttering, "And here we go." He locked eyes with Taylor. "Tay, look... you know I love you in a completely nonsexual-keep-it-in-your-pants kind of way, but you really gotta let this go, man. It's going to drive you nuts, which is going to drive me nuts in return. I can't afford the distraction, and you can't afford to lose any more brain cells."

Taylor looked up at him. He knew Benny was right, but he also knew he couldn't, no, he *wouldn't* give up Jackson. Which he had to admit was weird, since he didn't actually have Jackson in the first place.

WHEN the first bell rang on Monday morning, Taylor was already at his desk. He looked around for Jackson but hadn't yet seen him. He was trembling with anticipation, dying to know why Jackson had been at his door. Becca came strolling in a minute later, Jackson on her arm. She shot Taylor a withering glance and put her hand on the small of Jackson's back, walking him to his desk before going to her own. Taylor didn't understand what was going on, but he was determined to ask Jackson why he'd been over to his house. He got up and headed for the baseball star's desk. He didn't make it very far, as Becca jumped out of her seat and intercepted him. She grabbed his sleeve and dragged him to the back of the class. When Taylor tried to pull away, Becca tightened her grip, letting him know he had no choice.

"What are you doing?" she hissed.

"I need to talk to Jax, not that it's any of your business," Taylor replied, utterly confused as to why Becca was acting this way.

"Jax *is* my business, thank you," she said imperiously. "He's going to be pitching tonight, and he needs to concentrate. I won't have you ruin this for him with your stupid boy crush."

Taylor blinked a few times. He was stunned but recovered quickly.

"Excuse me? What the hell are you talking about?"

"I've seen the way you look at him. And let me tell you, it disgusts both of us," she snapped.

"What do you mean? I don't have a boy crush on him," he said, trying to keep his voice even, while looking around to see if anyone was listening. He couldn't have been more hurt if she had actually slapped him.

"We both know you do," she spat jabbing him in the chest. "He came over to your house on Saturday to tell you that he wanted you to stay away from him. He's grossed out by you. Do you get that?"

The bell rang, and both of them returned to their seats. Taylor's head spun, his palms were damp, and he couldn't catch his breath. He was going to have a freaking panic attack, he just knew it. He tried to focus on his breathing, willing himself to calm down. He knew the reason that Jax… Jackson, since they obviously weren't friends, had been at his house wasn't like his fantasy. God, how could he have been so stupid? And Becca knew he was gay? He wanted to curl up and cry, but he wasn't about to give either Jackson or the blonde viper the satisfaction. When the bell rang, he saw Jackson get up and start moving in his direction. Having already been humiliated, Taylor ran out the door and headed off to his first-period class. He knew that he'd stay away from Jackson. He knew that without a doubt in his mind.

CHAPTER THREE
CAN'T STAY AWAY

THE game started late due to rain. It hadn't been a downpour, so the field was dry enough to play, but it was still kind of sloppy. Taylor couldn't for the life of him figure out why he was there. After he'd told Benny about his conversation with Becca, Benny made him promise to stay away. And he'd had every intention of doing so. Why, then, was he there, watching a game he had no interest in, being played by a guy who was disgusted by him?

When he saw Jackson, Taylor could feel the butterflies tickling his stomach. Jackson did his normal routine. He came out of the dugout and went to the mound, looked around and waved to everyone. Just like that, the butterflies went from fluttering wings to jackhammers. The batter stepped in, and Jackson went into his stance, throwing the first pitch of the game. Three innings later the team was ahead 4-0. Jackson was delivering blistering pitches, and he was completely baffling the Milwaukee Tech team. As the teams switched for the start of the fourth inning, Taylor felt a hand on his shoulder.

"Couldn't stay away, could you? I knew I'd find you here," Benny said somewhat sadly.

"I tried, Benny. I don't know why I'm out here," Taylor replied weakly. He turned to face his friend.

"Dude, you are so hopeless," Benny said with a small smile.

Taylor couldn't meet Benny's eyes when he answered. "I really thought he was different... I thought he was... I dunno, nice? Good? Kind? All of the above? He's not like anyone else I've met before."

Benny reached out and put a hand on Taylor's shoulder. "I don't know what to say. Guess you just don't know the real guy, huh? How about we leave, and I'll buy you an ice cream? Babe's has some great vegan flavors," Benny whispered, trying to soothe Taylor.

Taylor shook his head. He turned his attention to Benny and tried to force a smile. "No, you go ahead. I want to see how the game ends. Maybe next time, okay?"

"Sure, I understand. No problem. Catch you later," Benny mumbled, moving away. He stopped and turned back to Taylor. "Please don't let this take over your life," he pleaded softly before heading to the parking lot.

Taylor sighed. He knew Benny was looking out for him. He always had, ever since they were little. Benny had been more like a cool older brother than a friend. It was one of the things he liked best, their close bond. Being able to completely trust the guy without any kind of sexual feelings gumming up the works. And even though he was a complete brain, Benny was also really down-to-earth. Taylor couldn't count the number of times Benny had helped him with his schoolwork and projects. If it wasn't for Benny, he realized, he probably wouldn't be applying for colleges in two years. He knew Benny wouldn't be able to help him with this situation, though. He realized Jackson was something he needed to handle on his own, even if he had no idea how the hell to do it.

The game was a shutout. Milwaukee Tech had no chance, losing 11-0, dropping them to second place in the division. With only three more games in the regular season, it certainly seemed the boys would make it to state for the first time in twelve years.

With every victory Jackson's reputation increased, Becca became more possessive, and Taylor grew more anxious.

NEAR the end of the season, the student body held elections to determine who would lead the class in the next year. Traditionally a senior held the role, but Jackson Kern, probably the most popular person in school, was the overwhelmingly nominated write-in candidate for Student Council President. When the votes were tallied, he had won a landslide victory. Next year he would be the youngest student council president in the school's history.

An assembly was held to introduce the class to the new student council. When Jackson strode to the podium, he had a smile lighting his entire face. Dressed in a charcoal gray suit, he was striking. Taylor was awed. He couldn't help but be dazzled by the young man's confidence, charm, and dynamic energy.

"My name is Jackson Kern. Most of you probably already know me as the pitcher for the baseball team that's heading to the state finals," he shouted.

There were raucous cheers by the excited classmates. Jackson waited for everyone to calm down, a faint smile on his face.

"I can't tell you how honored I am you elected me as the student council president," Jackson said quietly, gazing out at the student body. "This means so much to me. When I was growing up, we moved around a lot. It made it difficult to make friends, because we never knew how long we'd be in one spot. My mom died when I was a kid, and it made it even more difficult because—" His voice broke. "Well, you know how moms are."

It took a moment for him to gain his composure before he was able to continue.

"I've been in a lot of different places, and each one was so different. There were towns where football was almost a religion. Some towns it was wrestling. In some places academics were the rule, believe it or not. I never had the opportunity to fit in, because I never knew what to expect when I got there."

He paused briefly to glance down at his note cards.

"I'm a baseball player, but that's not all I am. I'm good at math and science. I love to read. I know how to play chess. Those things together make up a part of who I am. I don't like the labels. As the student council president I want everyone's opinion, not just those I agree with. Tell me what you think, because we all see the world differently and having other opinions will go a long way to making things better for everyone. I want our school to be a welcoming place for all of us. I want people to be able to come here and fit in, no matter who they are. I want it to be a safe haven for every student. I want us to become more than a school. I'd like us to be a community."

For a moment there was quiet, and then the applause began, building to a thunderous standing ovation.

Taylor looked at his classmates. Some of them were brought to tears by Jackson's speech. Taylor knew, with the popularity Jackson had, if anyone could do it, he'd be the man. He did have to wonder, though, how Jackson would deal with any kinds of gay issues, seeing as how he was disgusted by a gay guy, but he opted not to dwell on it. Maybe it was just him Jackson had the issue with and not gay people in general.

WITH only two games left in the regular season, the team was still undefeated, having notched only one close call. No matter how much he wanted to stay away, Taylor always found himself in the same spot each game. One moment he'd tell himself he simply wasn't going to go to the game, but somehow he still found himself there before the first pitch was thrown. He was going to be really glad when baseball season was over. Perhaps then he could finally deal with his crush over a guy who couldn't stand him. Maybe he'd actually be able to move on and get back to normal. Maybe pigs would fly too, but hope springs eternal.

The last game of the season finally rolled around. The team had already clinched the division and would be going to the state competition. The coach made the decision to put the guys who didn't see much playing time during most of the season in for the final game. It was a tight game, but they still came out on top. A perfect season, division champs, the tournament trophy. Jackson was the golden boy. In fact, he was so high on top, Becca hadn't dumped him at the end of the season like she normally would any other player. As long as Jackson's star was rising, so was hers. Taylor had this recurring image of the two of them after high school, getting married, having 2.5 children and a dog named Bitsy. A big house. Jackson had a great-paying job, maybe a doctor. Becca would be the homemaker. They'd live happily ever after. And even though Taylor wished it could be the life he could have with Jackson, he still didn't begrudge him—well, not much. He wanted him happy, even if it meant Becca got to be happy too. Of course Taylor also fantasized he was seeing Jackson on the side, but that was neither here nor there.

The Wisconsin State Baseball Spring Tournament Finals would be played at Fox Cities Stadium in Appleton. The team had made it through the quarter and semifinals with no problems. Jackson would be pitching for the final against Milwaukee King. Seeing as how it was a little more than a hundred miles away, Taylor wanted to set out early so he could stake out his usual spot. He'd asked Benny to come along but was told there was a science project due on Monday he needed to finish.

"You *did* do the project, right, Tay?" Benny groaned.

"Oh sure, of course. I had it done Friday," Taylor hedged, trying to be as vague as possible since he didn't even remember there was a project.

"Taylor, this is our year-end project. It counts for 50 percent of our grade. You have to make sure it's done."

Taylor was already calculating. If he made this trip, it would take him about two hours to get there and two hours to get home. The game would last a couple of hours. There just wasn't any way he'd be able to pull off the project in time. He was so screwed.

"Benny, what kind of project are we supposed to do?" he asked quietly.

Benny sighed heavily. Taylor knew his friend was irritated because he'd let his priorities get so messed up. Benny had always pushed him to make sure he got his work done on time because, Benny said, he didn't want to be going off to college alone, and Taylor had to come with him. Taylor knew he got decent grades, but if he bombed this science project he'd likely fail the course for the year, and that would affect his transcripts. Sure, he was only going to be a junior, but he needed to buckle down and pull up his GPA if he wanted to get into any school Benny would be going to, because his friend was like crazy smart.

"Look, it's not that simple." Benny gave an exasperated huff. "This project takes weeks to complete, man. You were supposed to be doing mold experiments: Do different types of bread grow different types of mold? Does temperature or light affect the growth of mold? This isn't something you can do in two days."

Taylor's heart sank. He was toast and he knew it. He knew he'd been letting his schoolwork slide, but he had been so wrapped up in his obsession for Jackson it hadn't really seemed to matter.

"I'm sorry, Benny. I screwed up big time. I'll go to summer school to make up for this, I promise. I'll talk with Mr. Dean on Monday morning."

Benny rubbed the bridge of his nose, obviously trying to cover up his frustration. "You're an idiot, Tay. A stone-cold, in-over-your-head idiot. You know that, right?"

"Yes," Taylor replied weakly. He knew it, all right.

Benny let out a sigh. "I'm thinking the project I did for you should get you a B. Is that good enough?"

Taylor couldn't believe he was hearing this right. "What? What are you talking about?"

"I did two projects, Tay," Benny told him, his voice tight. "One for me, one for you. I've seen how you've been lately, and I knew you weren't working on your project. I could get you an A, but I'm thinking Mr. Dean would realize it wasn't your work."

Taylor didn't even have to consider the next words that came out of his mouth. "No, thank you. It'd be cheating and neither of us cheats," he said with more confidence than he actually felt. "I'll do the summer school and, hopefully, get my head on straight. I'm really sorry I put you in this position, Benny."

"You gotta know I'd do it for you. I wouldn't like it, but I'd do it. Because you're important to me." Benny sounded like he was stressed and having difficulty saying it.

Taylor met Benny's gaze and wouldn't look away. "That's why I won't let you do it, Benny. It would make you lose respect for me, and sometimes that's all I have."

"God, I swear... if you were a girl, you would so be mine," Benny said quietly.

Taylor laughed. "You could always come over to the dark side, dude."

"The thing is, sometimes, if I could, I think I'd do it just so I could be with you," came the whispered answer.

Taylor had no reply. He knew his friend was serious, and he was humbled. Benny told Taylor he should go ahead and go to the game. Since he didn't have the project, and there was no way for him to get it done (and despite Benny offering him the second project again, Taylor continued to refuse), he should try to enjoy the day.

The drive to Appleton wasn't difficult. Pretty much a straight shot down Highway 41 to the stadium. The place was packed when Taylor arrived. He made his way to the bleachers and blanched when he saw Becca. He considered finding somewhere else to sit but decided there was no way he would let her run his life. He camped in his usual spot, watching Jackson warming up. He knew Jackson was a great pitcher, but today the man moved like quicksilver. One strong, fluid motion. It was breathtaking to see, and Taylor was drawn to sketch it. When the game commenced, Jackson did his usual: run out to the field, look to *her*, and give a smile and wave to the audience. Taylor groaned, wishing he could either talk with the man or just leave, but it wasn't going to happen. He didn't feel strong enough to do either. Maybe summer school would be good for him.

The game was a nail-biter. Jackson had held King scoreless, but their pitcher had done the same. In the bottom half of the ninth inning, Mitch Daniels hit a high, towering home run. It was a beautiful shot, and as soon as it cracked off the bat, everyone knew the game was over and the team had won their division. Screaming fans poured out onto the field, holding Mitch and Jackson on their shoulders. It was a great moment and one Taylor hoped to remember for the rest of his life. The looks on the team members' faces was worth it. When they put Jackson down, he was immediately grabbed up by Becca, who hugged and kissed him on the side of the mouth. Taylor was glad to see Jackson succeed. After hearing about how difficult life was for Jackson with the constant moving around, Taylor was very pleased that maybe Jackson had finally found somewhere he might settle down. Taylor was so happy he didn't even hate Becca... much.

MONDAY morning Taylor found his parents in the kitchen. He steeled himself before sitting down at the table.

"Mom? Dad? Can I talk with you for a couple minutes?" His palms got damp when his parents' attention fixed on him.

"Of course, Taylor. What's going on?" his mom asked.

Taylor sighed and pushed his palm against his eye. *Better just get it over with....*

"I'm going to be talking to Mr. Dean, my science teacher, today. I—um—didn't do a project for him. It was a really important one, and without it I'm going to flunk the class. I'm going to be asking him to let me take the course for summer school."

He watched his parents, trying to gauge their reaction. They were quiet for several moments as they considered his words.

"Why didn't you do the project? What was going on that you couldn't do it?" his mother demanded to know.

Taylor sucked in a breath. He couldn't tell them about Jackson, but what other excuse could he possibly give them?

"I... I've been distracted by someone. I really like them, and I was trying to get them to notice me. It kinda messed up my priorities." He glanced up at them, not wanting to meet their gaze. Finally his father spoke, his words measured.

"We're glad you've accepted responsibility, Taylor. We're very disappointed you let this happen, though. If it wasn't for the fact you're going to be doing summer school, you know there'd be a grounding in there, right?" his father told him in no uncertain terms.

"Yeah, Dad, I know. I'm really sorry," Taylor replied. He looked down at the table as tears pricked his eyes. He could deal with the grounding, but to disappoint his parents really sucked.

His mom put her arms around him. "We still love you. You do know that, right? We want what's best for you."

He nodded, not trusting himself to speak.

"Do you need us to come see Mr. Dean with you?" she asked, kissing his forehead.

Taylor straightened his back and looked her in the eye. "No thanks, Mom. I messed up, and I'm the one who'll have to fix it. I appreciate it, though."

His dad clapped him on the shoulder, and his mom hugged him. He felt a lot better when he headed off to school.

TAYLOR stood at the door to the classroom and saw Daryl Dean sitting at his desk. Mr. Dean was a big man, nearly as tall as Benny, with a barrel chest and booming voice. He was in his thirties, definitely handsome, with hazel eyes, sandy hair, and a goatee. Taylor always enjoyed his class. Mr. Dean referred to everyone as Mr. or Ms., never by his or her first name, something Taylor found somewhat charming. He knocked at the door to announce himself. "Mr. Dean? I was wondering if you had a minute?"

"Of course, Mr. Andrews. You're here quite early," Mr. Dean said, taking a peek at his watch. "What can I do for you?" he asked, obviously surprised to see *anyone* so early in the morning.

"I… I needed to talk to you about the project we have due. I didn't get it done, sir."

"I see. Was the assignment too difficult, Mr. Andrews?"

"No, sir. I failed to do it. I have no excuses. I was hoping to talk to you about making the class up during summer school, if I can?"

Mr. Dean stared at Taylor for a few moments. "Mr. Andrews, in all my years of teaching I've never had anyone approach me like this. I have to admit, I find it quite refreshing. I must say you've surprised me. This doesn't happen often. Generally I get sob stories or people begging me for more time. You've shown a remarkable amount of maturity in coming to me. Up until today your work has been exemplary. You've maintained good grades and high standards at all times."

He paused for a moment, ensuring he had Taylor's attention. "While I can't let you off the hook for this, I can, however, offer you an opportunity. You'll be given additional time to finish your project; in return you'll need to do something for me."

Mr. Dean paused again. Taylor could see the man's hands were beginning to shake, and his voice seemed choked with emotion. The teacher removed his glasses and swiped a hand across his eyes before he continued. "My son, Adrian... Addy, will be going to a summer camp for abused children. We adopted him when he was eight. He is sixteen now. His father... hurt him, badly, for more than two years, doing things that still cause Addy nightmares. Each year my son goes to this camp, they want the campers to talk to survivors of abuse, peer counselors, and other campers, but Addy never participates. Every year he comes back just as he was when he left. He's never willing to let anyone in. They need volunteers for the summer, and I would appreciate it if you could be one of them. It would be a good volunteer opportunity and would look good on a college application. It probably won't be easy. Addy is a wonderful kid, but very withdrawn."

Taylor knew Mr. Dean was baiting him, trying to... not necessarily blackmail, but leverage him into going. Thing was, he only needed to ask.

"Mr. Dean, I'm happy to do it. It sounds like just the thing I need this summer. And I appreciate you giving me the time to finish the project," Taylor said respectfully.

Mr. Dean gave Taylor the information he'd need to volunteer at the camp, located near the border of the Upper Peninsula of

Michigan. He'd leave at the end of June, giving him a couple of weeks to do his project, and he'd be gone for about two and a half months. When he saw Benny, he told him about what Mr. Dean had done, and Benny surprised him by offering to come along to help out.

"He's right, you know. It would be good on a college application. And it'd give me time with my best friend. Win-win, I figure."

Taylor looked around, saw no one in the area, and gave Benny a quick hug. He started to pull back when Benny grabbed him and held him tight.

"You'll always be my bestie, Tay. Always."

Taylor had to wipe his eyes quick before Benny let go. He must have gotten some dust in them or something, because they were watering like crazy.

.

CHAPTER FOUR

CAMP IT UP

TAYLOR turned in the project—he actually earned a B+ on it—the weekend before he and Benny left for Camp Care, the sixty-acre spread where kids who had been abused could get together, do activities, speak with counselors, and be normal kids for a while. The camp was beautiful. A large copse of evergreen trees scented the air; the lake was a brilliant blue, reflecting a bright sun, with just a slight ripple caused by the warm wind. This year the camp would welcome eighteen campers and thirty-six counselors, two for each camper. The counselors were warned some of the children had serious physical and emotional scars. Some of them could be friendly one moment, brutally angry the next. Some of them never spoke about their abuse, feeling they'd somehow caused it, leaving them with an overwhelming sense of guilt. In short, none of these kids should ever be treated as anything other than individuals. Many of them were rebuilding their lives and were, at best, tenuous. The camp counselor's job was to keep them happy, motivated, and cared for. To show them not everyone wanted to hurt them. To show there were still caring people in the world. The counselors were also warned some kids might share information about their abuse, and each of them should be ready to deal with the aftermath such revelations might bring. This was going to be an emotionally exhausting summer.

When Taylor and Benny were introduced to Addy Dean, the first thing Taylor noticed was the young man looked haunted. His brown eyes were deep-set and constantly scanning. When one of the canoes banged against the dock and made a loud, hollow thump, Addy flinched and covered his ears. He wore a long-sleeved shirt buttoned up completely. His dark-blond hair was pretty shaggy, dropping to just below his collar. His face was pale and thin, making him look much smaller than his five-foot-five-inch frame.

"Hi, Addy, or do you prefer Adrian?" Taylor asked, extending his hand.

"Addy is fine," the boy mumbled, just staring at the outstretched hand. Taylor pulled the hand back. He nodded toward his friend.

"This is Benny. He and I are going to be your counselors while you're at the camp."

"Fine," Addy replied, seemingly uninterested in further conversation. Taylor looked to Benny and gave a slight shrug.

"Do you want to go to the cabin, Addy?" Benny asked.

"I guess."

Benny and Taylor exchanged panicked glances but said nothing. They took the boy's luggage and showed him where he'd be staying for the next twelve weeks. Addy threw his suitcase on the floor and flopped on the lower bunk.

"Why are you here?" he asked, his eyes cold and his tone equally harsh.

"What do you mean?" Taylor replied, glancing toward Benny

"Daryl... my adopted dad, told me you were going to be here with me. I want to know why. What did he do to get you here?" he demanded, his attitude unchanged.

"He asked" was Taylor's simple reply.

"Right. He just asked you to work with me, and you jumped at the chance," Addy sneered.

"Honestly? Yeah. I'd messed up. I asked him about doing summer school. He asked me if I'd be interested in working here for the summer instead," Taylor replied, embarrassed at having to admit his failure.

"So you didn't really want to come here, right? How about you just leave me alone and I'll tell him you were great and we can all just stay out of each other's way?" Addy glared at Taylor, trying to stare him down.

Benny regarded him with narrowed eyes. "Well, I'm here because I want to be. Taylor is my best friend, has been since we were kids. I wanted the opportunity to work here for the summer."

Addy's mouth dropped open with a gasp. "Wait. You *want* to be here? Why the hell for?"

"What do you mean? This looks like a decent place. What's wrong with it?" Taylor huffed.

"Nothing is wrong with the place. It's the people. We're the screwups! We're the ones no one else wanted," he shrieked. He was quiet for a moment. When he spoke again Taylor had to strain to hear the words. "We're the ones who were so bad we needed to be punished."

Benny bristled. Clearly he'd had enough. "Addy, stop. Mr. Dean wanted you. He didn't have to adopt you. He chose to do it. Taylor and I didn't have to be here. We wanted to. No one forced us."

"Usually the guys that come here are only interested in meeting the girls. They're not here for anything else."

A smile split Taylor's face. "Well, that might be something up Benny's alley."

Benny smacked him in the arm. Addy looked at them and actually gave a slight smile. It was then Taylor knew it'd be an okay time for all of them. When he told Addy to change and they'd go out to the lake, Addy said he was fine the way he was.

Benny laughed. "Little man, it's going to be way too hot out there. Change into some shorts, and we'll take you down for a little swimming before we go to dinner."

"Come on, Addy, we'll have some fun. Maybe we can take one of the boats out or something," Taylor coaxed, trying to get him to loosen up.

Addy shook his head violently. "I don't do shorts. I don't take my shirt off. I'm fine the way I am."

Not wanting to push the boy, Taylor backed off. "Okay, what do you want to do?"

"Can we just talk for a while?" Addy pleaded.

Benny and Taylor glanced at each other and motioned to some chairs in the cabin, where they all sat down. Addy asked them to tell him about themselves. Benny smiled and began to tell him the story of their first meeting.

"We were in kindergarten," Benny recalled. "Taylor was pitching a fit because he didn't want to do nap time. The teacher was getting way annoyed with him, but he just wouldn't lie down."

"It's not my fault. I'd had chocolate milk and needed to pee," Taylor interjected at this point. Benny smirked and went on with the story.

"Yeah, but you didn't tell her that. You just got all cranky. Anyway, he was being an annoying ass, refusing to lie down, and suddenly he just froze. The teacher looked at him, and he started crying. Hard."

Heat flooded Taylor's cheeks. "I peed my pants."

Addy snickered, gazed slyly at Benny, who waggled his eyebrows, and they both broke out laughing.

"Benny came to my rescue," Taylor said fondly. "He helped me to the bathroom while they called my mom for a change of clothes. He helped me get cleaned up, and he got me calmed down. The teacher handed him some clothes for me, and he helped me get changed. He never said a word about it, just acted like nothing had happened. I knew right then he was going to be my best friend."

Addy's smile faded a bit as he seemed to consider his counselors' story. "That's really cool," he said, his voice soft. "I wish I had a friend like that."

Taylor cringed. He had hoped the story would give Addy something to smile about, not another thing to make him sad. He looked to Benny, hoping his friend would say something to break the tension.

"What about you, Addy? What's your story?"

As soon as the question was out, Taylor could see Benny regretted it. Addy's face contorted. He shot off the bed and ran out the door, followed closely by Taylor, who called out to him.

"Addy, stop. We're sorry. We didn't mean it like that. We were just having a good time and forgot about why we were here."

Addy stopped, his breathing rapid. He turned and looked at Taylor, as if trying to judge from his words whether they were true or not. Taylor hoped the young man would see his sincerity.

"I'm sorry," Addy whispered.

Taylor stepped forward and went to put his hand on Addy's shoulder, only to pause when the young man flinched. He pulled his hand back and looked into Addy's eyes, desperately wanting him to see they'd meant no harm.

"Addy, we don't know what happened to you, and we're not really sure what you're comfortable with, but if you could just talk with us and let us know, it'd probably be easier for everyone."

Addy stood for a moment and shuffled his feet. He gave a hesitant nod and stumbled back toward the cabin.

When they returned Benny came rushing toward them, rubbing the back of his neck. "Addy, I'm sorry, I didn't mean—"

"It's cool," Addy cut Benny off. Addy looked away, fingers fidgeting with the buttons on his shirt. "I don't want to talk about why I'm here. Even Daryl doesn't know the whole story, and it's not something I think I can talk about. I don't like to be touched, and I only wear pants and long-sleeved shirts. Can we just let it go at that?"

"Sure, that's cool. We'll start with that."

They sat for a time in awkward silence. When the bell rang for dinner, they headed to the mess hall. Taylor kept an eye on Addy, noticing how hesitant he seemed when they were around other people. He noticed Addy tugging his sleeves, making sure they were pulled to his hands, and how he seemed nervous when the conversations grew louder. Taylor knew there was something on Addy's mind, and he wished he could figure out a way to comfort the obviously uncomfortable young man.

THE first evening they turned in early, exhausted from the travel. Taylor shifted to his side when he heard a soft noise coming from inside the cabin. The moon cast a light glow, allowing him to see the other beds. He heard a sniffle and a low, aching moan. Reaching out, he nudged Benny awake and pointed toward Addy's bunk. The two of them moved quietly toward their camper's bed. Addy was tossing, tears running down his cheeks. He had the covers pulled tightly to his chin, like he was trying to shield himself from something. He groaned, his eyes flew open, and he screamed. Addy's chest was heaving, his breath coming in ragged gasps. His face took on a pained look, and his eyes went wide. He seemed frightened and extremely agitated. Taylor sat on the bed and started rubbing Addy's back while Benny whispered to him soothingly, letting him know everything was okay.

The other campers were awakened by the keening sound and gathered around to see what was going on. Their counselors urged them to step back and give Addy some room.

"Addy? Look at me, okay?" Taylor pleaded as his hand moved in slow, comforting circles on Addy's back.

Addy drew the covers up even tighter. He seemed locked into the nightmare he was experiencing. Taylor met Benny's eyes, hoping his friend would be able to do something to help.

"Hey, little man," Benny's smooth voice coaxed as he went to his knees beside the bed. "Why don't you relax? Just relax," he murmured.

Benny's voice seemed to have a calming effect on Addy, as his breathing slowed and the panicked look in his eyes faded. Addy blinked a couple of times before he was back in the moment.

"You okay, little man?" Benny asked, the concern obvious in his voice.

"Wh-where am I?" Addy managed to ask, his eyes locked on Benny's.

"You're at camp with Taylor and me. Remember? Addy, I need you to remember, okay?"

Addy gazed around the room slowly. "Oh God, I haven't had one of those in a long time," he admitted.

"What happened, Addy? Are you all right?"

It was obviously the wrong question. Addy's mouth clamped shut. He glared at his counselors, rolled over, and dragged the covers back to his chin.

"I'm fine," he muttered. "Leave me alone."

Taylor could tell by Benny's expression he was just as stunned by what had happened, but they both went back to their cots. Sleep didn't come easily after that.

THE first week went by achingly slow. Addy just couldn't seem to warm up to either Benny or Taylor and seemed to grow more sullen and withdrawn. During the start of the second week, they were going to be doing some art classes. Addy stubbornly refused to go.

"Why? Art is awesome," Benny told him.

"I can't draw" was the reply.

"Tay can. You should see his stuff. It's amazing."

Addy shot a questioning glance at Taylor, who shrugged in reply.

"Don't let him fool you, Addy. Taylor has the makings of a great artist. Why not come with us and see what he can do?"

Addy grudgingly agreed to go along. They made their way to the rec center, set up with easels and supplies stationed throughout the room. The other campers were with their counselors, drawing, painting, and arguing. Taylor grabbed an easel and set it up, keeping an eye on Addy. He began to draw. His hands flew over the paper, capturing the essence of the younger man, a fleeting smile, the way his eyes shone. When he was done, Addy stepped over and inspected the finished project.

"That's… me?" he asked, eyes wide.

"Yeah, at least how I see you," Taylor replied.

Addy stared at the drawing, his head shaking softly. "But I'm nothing like that. I'm—" He paused, trying to find the right words. "—not beautiful," he muttered, his hands gliding over his shirtsleeves.

"Yeah, you are. Why would you doubt it?"

Addy worried his bottom lip with his teeth before he beckoned for Taylor and Benny to follow him. He went to the far corner of the room, out of sight of the other campers, closed his eyes, and started unbuttoning his long-sleeved shirt. Taylor and Benny both gasped as the boy slid the garment off his slender frame. Deep scars crisscrossed his arms, burn marks evident in several places across them as well. He lifted his T-shirt and revealed even more deep scars and burn marks.

"I have other ones in places no one is going to see," he informed them as he tucked in his shirt again. "My dad told me I was a screwup," he whispered. "He told me I deserved to be punished. He said I was worthless. He used to beat me with a cord if I did something he didn't like. I broke a glass once, and he beat me so bad I couldn't sit down. He used to think it was funny when he burned me. He'd put his cigarettes out on me, and when I screamed he'd tell me I had to man up, and that I was a punk if I couldn't handle it. He told me it was out of love for me that he did it. He told me it was love that made him… do other stuff to me. I hated him so bad, but I loved him too, ya know? I mean, he was my dad."

Addy couldn't seem to stop the tears welling in his eyes from spilling over.

Taylor grimaced, figuring both he and Benny knew what "stuff" the boy was talking about, but they'd have to talk with one of the head counselors about that. How the hell could a man do something like that? To his own son? Taylor had the sudden urge to call his own dad and just say thank you.

Taylor had a realization. "Addy," Taylor wondered aloud, "is that what you were dreaming about the other night?"

Addy nodded slowly. "I haven't had a dream that bad for a long time. When Daryl adopted me, I used to have them nearly every night. I'd wake up him and Celia, his wife, and they'd always be there to calm me down. They sent me to therapy, but I didn't really want to talk about what happened, and after a while I just refused to go. I thought it was getting better but...."

"Addy, what your... what he did to you was all kinds of wrong. No one deserves that. Ever," Benny said harshly. "You're a great guy. Mr. Dean even said so. They just want to know how to help you. Whatever you need, they'd be there for you," Benny reminded him.

"I know. He's always been amazing, and I've acted like a shit. I'm really sorry about it, but I get so mad all the time. I do something wrong and expect the punishment that never comes. It's like they don't love me because they don't...." He dropped his eyes, refusing to look at Taylor or Benny.

"Because he won't beat you? Because he won't hurt you?" Benny asked softly.

Addy simply nodded.

"Little man," Benny said, "I'm sorry, but your biological dad was a prick. My parents are constantly on me, telling me I need to be the best, but I'm not perfect, and they've never been anything but proud of me, even when I disappoint them. What your biological father did was not love. It was degrading and hurtful." Benny's voice sounded strained, as if he was having a hard time controlling his anger. "Love is what Mr. Dean is giving you. The chance to explore your feelings. The chance to try and come to terms with what happened to you. None of this stuff should have happened to anyone, but especially not to you. I don't know why your biological father did what he did, but I promise you it was not out of love. Stop giving him the power to control you," Benny said forcefully.

Taylor put his finger under Addy's chin, surprised when he didn't pull away. Taylor tilted Addy's head up and looked him in the eye. "Do you know why I like art?"

Addy shook his head.

"It's an outlet. My anger. My frustration. My jealousy. My love. My sadness. All pulled down to a pure feeling I unleash on the canvas. I've drawn pictures of Benny I look at when I'm sad, because he makes me so happy. I draw pictures of Ja—someone else because I like them so much, but I'm afraid to tell them. Every time I do a sketch, it's because of an emotion. Some sweet, some harsh. That's what art is to me. You just need to lose yourself in the picture."

Addy considered his words, returned to their station, and cautiously picked up a paintbrush. "What should I do?" he asked.

"Whatever feels right to you. Let it out through your painting."

The first few strokes were hesitant, testing. Bright, joyous colors against the virgin white background. Then the deeper strokes became bold whorls of black and red, angry strokes of color blotting out the others. Addy gazed at the canvas, his face contorted, tears leaking from his eyes. He started slashing at it with the paintbrush, savage imagery in his mindscape brought to bear on the artwork. Over and over Addy thrust the brush, and the more he did it, the more wild-eyed he got. When he was finished, he slumped in the chair, exhausted. He stared at what he'd done, his face still contorted, his chest heaving. Taylor and Benny said nothing, simply watching him for a time.

"Addy," Taylor whispered, a knowing grin creeping across his face. "That was awesome. This is some of the neatest stuff I've ever seen."

Addy looked up at Taylor, a slight smile spreading across his face, chasing back the shadows. "Seriously?" He paused. "Do you want it?" he asked softly.

"Really? I would be honored to have an Addy Dean original," Taylor exclaimed, ruffling the boy's hair, frowning just a bit when Addy flinched.

Small steps, he told himself.

AFTER that day Addy seemed to open up, little by little. Though he still refused to take his shirt off in front of other people, he rolled up the sleeves when just Taylor and Benny were around. He also loosened the top button, allowing just a peek of neck to show through. Not to say there weren't bad days. One day during an art class, Addy accidentally tipped over his easel, knocking brushes and paints to the floor. He looked defiantly at his counselors, daring them to do something. Taylor bent and picked up the easel, while Benny began cleaning the paint. No recriminations, no shouting. Taylor could see it confused Addy, and his face twisted with anger because, again, he waited for a punishment that would never come, as if his whole life depended on being chastised. When he realized it wasn't going to happen, he deflated and said, "Sorry," very softly and started to help Benny.

After the first month, Addy refused to take part in any other camp activities. All he wanted to do was paint. He seemed to lose bits of rage every time he completed a piece. He'd work on art projects with Taylor, and afterward he would wander around and talk with Benny. Those talks seemed to go on and on. He became more open and vocal with Taylor and Benny, telling them about his life with the Deans. Talking about the family he grew up with. They learned so much about his life, and they were impressed he was so strong. Both Taylor and Benny agreed had it been either of them, they doubted they would have survived Addy's ordeal. When they told one of the head counselors about the conversation where Addy alluded to sexual abuse, he promised he'd speak with the Deans about getting Addy some more professional help. He also commented on how, over the course of the last few years, Addy had never let anyone in enough to talk about the abuse, and how he and Benny must be some really special guys if they were able to get Addy to open up. They blushed at the praise.

By the end of the summer, the boys were physically and emotionally exhausted. Mr. Dean came to pick up Addy, who raved about things they'd done, how he hoped Taylor and Benny would come back next year. The most surprising thing, though, was when he put his arms around his adoptive father and said very clearly, "Thank you, Dad." The look on Mr. Dean's face at the simple words spoke volumes. After packing up the car and getting ready to leave, Taylor and Benny were surprised when they turned and found Addy behind them.

"Daryl... my dad told me I could come and say good-bye to you."

He looked down at his feet, toeing the edge of the grass, before he launched himself into Benny's arms and squeezed for all he was worth. Benny stood stiffly for a moment, as though unsure how to react. When it seemed like it was okay, he put his arms around his charge, lowered his head, and whispered in the boy's ear, "Little dude, I've learned so much from you this summer. I can't tell you how grateful I am to have met you." Addy squeezed even harder, as if afraid to let go.

When Addy finally released Benny, he turned to Taylor and put his arms around him, soft and gentle, buried his face into Taylor's chest, and whispered, "Thank you for everything." He stepped back and looked at Taylor's face, then pulled him down by his shoulders and kissed him softly on the cheek. No other words were spoken. He turned and ran back to the car, waiting for his father to take him home.

Mr. Dean strode over to Taylor and Benny and extended his hand. "I am not sure what you did," he said, his eyes watering slightly, "but thank you so much. The counselor told me what Addy spoke with you about. It was always assumed he was abused—sexually—by his father, but Addy refused to ever talk about it. We hope now he can actually continue healing instead of holding it in. I owe you both so much, and honestly, I know I can never repay it."

"You already did, Mr. Dean," Taylor assured him. "It was a true pleasure, sir. Addy is an amazing guy. It might help if you could set him up with some art supplies. I think they help him to express his feelings a little better than he can any other way."

Mr. Dean regarded Taylor with a thoughtful expression. "Mr. Andrews, though I am not able to make a promise to you, I would like you to come and see me soon. I think I might have something of interest to you. You as well, Mr. Peters. Will you both give me your word that you'll come see me?"

Both agreed. Each shook Mr. Dean's hand, Benny gave Addy a wave and a wink, and they got ready for the long trip home.

BY THE time they'd returned home, they had a week left of summer vacation. Benny and Taylor got together several times during the week to talk about the camp. Benny asked Taylor to head over to the park with him and toss around a Frisbee. Taylor agreed, wanting to enjoy a little sunshine before school started up again.

"You going back next summer, Tay?" Benny wondered aloud.

"I think I'd like that. I always knew what art meant to me. I never really thought about what it could mean to someone else."

"Yeah, this summer really got me thinking about what I want to do with the rest of my life. We really made an impact, I think. We actually had an effect on someone's life. That's pretty freaking heady."

"I know," Taylor replied excitedly. They'd had a long conversation about Addy Dean during the four-hour drive back to Milwaukee. They took turns driving. While Taylor drove, Benny flipped through the sketchbook, seeing the world through Taylor's eyes, occasionally pausing to ask his friend about a particular sketch. Taylor could tell from the way Benny was talking he was happy, nervous, excited. A big jumble of emotions. Taylor, on the other hand, was remarkably calm. Art had always had a huge impact on his life, but to see the changes it made in Addy's life was, indeed, heady.

He'd drawn several pictures of Addy over the summer. The newer ones showed him, scars and all, as a much happier young man than he'd been. He hadn't shown them to anyone except Benny. It was like a terrible secret he wanted… or, perhaps, needed to share, but didn't trust anyone else to let in on it. Benny froze at the last picture. The one showing Benny and Addy hugging. The emotions on their faces had almost brought Taylor to tears.

Benny gasped when he saw the picture. "Do you… do you think I could have this? I mean, I know you drew it for you, but I really—"

"I did it for you, Benny. I know the summer meant a lot to you."

"More than you realize, Tay. I've never had an experience like that before. I wanted to protect him so bad. If I could go back in time and fix the problems, I really would."

"Yeah, I know what you mean. How could anyone do that to someone they claim to love? I know there's stuff that happened we don't know about, but—"

"No!" Benny spat out. "There's no excuse. Ever. He beat him, Taylor. He hurt him so badly the boy wanted to die. There is nothing that piece of garbage can ever do or say to justify it."

Taylor was taken aback by his friend's outburst. He'd never seen Benny so worked up. Benny was always the logical one, the voice of reason when others were flying off the handle. The look on his face was one of a man who would seriously compromise his own principles and react violently to protect someone else.

PITCH

CHAPTER FIVE
HOME AGAIN

THE first day back at school chaos reigned, pure and simple. Taylor dashed into homeroom and plopped down at his desk. The whole summer was a happy blur to him. On the ride home from camp, he'd realized he had been so busy he'd barely had time to give more than a passing thought to Jackson Kern and figured he could finally move on with his life. That lasted until Jackson ambled into class. Emotions dropped on Taylor like a shroud. Jackson obviously had been busy that summer. He was tanned and looked even more buff than ever. Taylor noticed Becca still trailing him. She must have clocked a lot of hours with him over the summer. Her complexion was radiant, smooth and soft, her tan every bit as deep as Jackson's. Taylor could feel the prickle of tears in his eyes as he picked up his sketchpad and thumbed through the pages, looking for a reminder of the truths he'd discovered over the summer, of things both important and benign.

"Good morning! Welcome back from vacation. Hope you all had a good time," Jackson said. "This year we're going to be doing some different events through the Student Council—a few dances, a carnival, and a few other things we hope will surprise and be well received. We're going to be looking for volunteers. I hope each of you will be able to give a little time to make the school a better place. If you'd like to help us out, there'll be sign-up sheets on the bulletin boards. We're really hoping to get some extra hands for dances, but we'd be happy to have you help out whenever you're able."

First day on the job as student council president and Jackson was already working on changes. Taylor decided it would be a good thing. He looked up at the charismatic young man's bright smile and all the flutters from last year came rushing back. He realized it wasn't just an infatuation or a crush. He was truly in love with this man.

Well, crap.

AFTER the last class of the day let out, Taylor found himself staring at all the sheets from the Student Council. Volunteers for dances, volunteers for the carnival they planned, volunteers for a wide variety of events. He signed up for all of them. When Benny found out, he just shook his head.

"Taylor, look, man, I don't want you to get so caught up like you did last year. It was almost a really bad situation, and you need some boundaries."

"Agreed, Benny. I promise you this year my schoolwork will come first."

"I should hope so, Mr. Andrews," a familiar voice started, "because I would like to talk with you and Mr. Peters, please."

Mr. Dean led the two friends to his classroom. It had been a week since they last saw him, but he seemed relaxed, happy.

"How's Addy, Mr. Dean?" Benny asked.

"He's doing well, Mr. Andrews," Mr. Dean replied, a broad smile lighting his face. "Thank you for asking. He's agreed to return to therapy, based on your recommendation to him, and the idea seems to agree with him. He's obviously let go of some of his anger, but there's still a lot of work to be done. It's not going to be an easy process, but we're going to work on it as a family. He's asked about both of you and wanted me to thank you for what you did for him."

"He's a very special guy," Benny said. "I'm really glad we got to know him."

"He speaks well of the two of you, also," Mr. Dean insisted. He placed his hands on the desk and leaned forward, the smile not diminished at all. "The reason I wanted you to come here today is I have a professor friend at the University of Vermont in Burlington. He works with what is referred to as Expressive Arts Therapy. Expressive arts therapies aim to heal individuals and groups and even promote positive social change. I believe the two of you would benefit from this program."

Taylor's jaw dropped. He'd never considered art as any kind of career, especially after being told by his father it was a wasted endeavor. This, though… this was tantalizing.

"I don't think it would do me much good, Mr. Dean," Benny stated. "I'm not an artist, and it's not really my thing. It's Taylor's."

"Yes, I know, Mr. Peters. However, Addy told me of your conversations with him. He told me while Mr. Taylor showed him how to express his emotions, you helped him to understand them. The University also has a great Integral Psychology program. I think this would be of benefit to you, if you think it might be something you would choose as a career path. I tell you this now, gentlemen, because it will require work on your part." Mr. Dean focused his attention on Benny. "Mr. Peters, you have very good grades, and I have no doubt you would do well in this program. Mr. Andrews, your grades are good, but you would need to take some courses that would allow you to step into this field. I believe the two of you, working together, could definitely make a go of this. If it would be of interest, of course."

Taylor and Benny looked at Mr. Dean and then at each other. Their faces broke into big smiles as a possible future path began to show itself.

"I've taken the liberty of getting information for the two of you. I trust you will avail yourselves of this chance, gentlemen. After you helped my son, I only feel it fair to tell you I think you each have great potential, and I would be disappointed to see you squander it."

THAT night Taylor and Benny went over the information Mr. Dean had given them. Both were excited about the possibility to do something to help others and to be doing something they enjoyed. Taylor wasn't hopeful, though, about talking to his parents. His dad had always told him he needed a career, that his art would never get him anywhere in life.

"Benny, what if he says no?" Taylor mumbled, picking at his fingernail. "What if he thinks it's stupid… that I'm stupid for even considering it?"

"Tay, your dad is a smart guy. Show him the information. Talk to him about what we did at camp. I'm sure he'll come up with the right answers."

"Thanks, Benny. Mr. Dean was right. You do know the right things to say. Addy was lucky to have you to talk to."

Benny grimaced. Taylor could see he was flustered. "Listen, Tay, about Addy… I… he…. You know what? Never mind. It's not important." Benny forced a smile. "So what's your plan to woo Jackson going to be this year?"

Taylor studied his friend curiously. Benny was never an evasive sort. He'd always worn his emotions proudly. Taylor decided to let it drop and talk about his favorite subject… at least for a while. "I don't have a plan. I mean, he's already made it pretty clear he's not into me. I volunteered for the committees to help him succeed, I guess. I know it sounds weak, but I figure if I help him, then maybe he could see we could be friends."

He expected Benny to roll his eyes or give him crap about his lusting again, but Benny regarded him expectantly for a moment and then said, "Yeah, Tay, I think that would be a great idea, as long as you remember to put your school stuff first this time. I want to check into this college thing, but I need you there with me."

"Agreed, but I'm going to need your help too. What Mr. Dean said was right. I need to bring my grades up. Do you think you could tutor me when I'm having problems?"

Benny put his hand on his friend's shoulder, giving it a gentle squeeze. "You don't even need to ask, man. I will always be there for you."

THAT weekend Taylor took the program information to his father. Taylor was nervous as hell when he asked if they could talk. His dad put down the paper and motioned to him to sit.

"What's up, Taylor? Everything okay?"

"Yeah, Dad." Taylor sat but shifted nervously in the chair. "I just need to talk to you about something. When we did the camp this summer, Benny and I met a kid named Addy who'd been abused by his father, really nasty stuff." Taylor paused for a moment and took in a deep breath. "We helped him, Dad. We got him to open up to us, to talk about stuff. Thing is, I helped him by talking about art. I know you always said it wasn't a career choice, but there's a school in Vermont that has a course where you learn to use art to affect social change, to help people like Addy. I know I'm probably going to disappoint you again, Dad, but Benny and I are talking about trying to do this. I like the idea of helping people, and if I can do it by using something I really like, well, I think that would be great."

Taylor held his breath, waiting for his dad to say something. Taylor could only hope his father could understand what he wanted to do, but he also realized the man was always so adamant against his art.

"I'm... sorry, Taylor."

That wasn't what Taylor wanted to hear. He knew his dad was going to continue on about how art was a bad choice. He peered up at his dad, watching as he wiped a hand across his face and gazed down at the table.

"Mr. Dean called me. He told me about how you helped his son and how much your artwork meant to the boy. I never meant to make you doubt yourself, Taylor. It was stupid of me. I should have encouraged your passion, not tried to rip it away from you. If this is what you want, then I will do my best to help you get it. I've seen your work. It's good. You're good. Really good."

50

Taylor's eyes went wide. "What?" he gasped. He never expected his father to change his mind. Taylor threw his arms around his father's waist and hugged him tight.

"Thank you, Dad. Really, thanks."

"I hope you know you can talk to us about anything, Taylor. Your mom and I love you. We will always love you. Nothing you can do will ever change that. No matter what, you'll always be our son," his father told him, returning the firm hug.

Taylor felt his face heat. He knew what he wanted to say to his dad, but couldn't bring himself to say it. Not now. Not today.

THE school held the tryouts for the baseball team. Jackson was on fire. The team looked to be every bit as solid, seeming to be ready to repeat as state champions. The coach told them they were the best team he'd seen take the field in a long while, even better than last year, as they had all their star players back plus a few really good prospects. Taylor found himself standing in his usual spot at practice again. Watching Jackson play was like a drug. It sent shivers through him watching Jackson's fluid grace. He always found it amusing that every time Jackson took the field, he'd wave at the crowd, just like it was a real game. He had heard baseball players were superstitious, and Jackson seemed determined to prove it. But, hey, if it worked for him....

The coach was right. The team did seem even better than it had last year. They worked together seamlessly, executing each play flawlessly. Taylor was impressed by the control Jackson displayed. He was confident, collected. He was the king of his domain and knew it. Thing was, though, when the newer players took the field he didn't lord it over them. He helped them. He guided them. He was helping to mold them into part of the team. Jackson was almost perfect. If it wasn't for that homophobia.... Taylor didn't want to think about it. Better he just show Jackson that, even though he was gay, he was a stand-up kind of guy. Someone you could go to in a pinch. He wanted to be Jackson's go-to guy, the one he would go to when he had a problem, the one he would turn to for advice. Taylor really just wanted to be everything for Jackson, and it hurt that he'd never have that opportunity.

THE first dance of the school year was the Halloween Spectacular. Jackson had been working on building up hype for the event, as it would be the first one for him as president. It had to go perfectly. Becca was in charge of putting the volunteers at their stations. Taylor got the refreshment table, which was, naturally, far enough away from the dance floor so he wouldn't be able to interact with anyone who didn't come to him first. Since it was a costume party, all the volunteers were expected to dress up. Taylor went as a baseball player. It amused Benny to no end.

"Dude, are you gonna try to show off your bat and balls?" he asked, laughing uproariously.

"Ha. Ha. It just seemed like the thing to do," Taylor replied. He didn't want to admit the outfit made him feel closer to Jackson.

"Well, I think you're freaking adorable, Tay." Benny laughed, reaching out and pinching one of his friend's pudgy cheeks.

The dance was in full swing. Taylor hadn't seen Jackson yet, but had been busy enough dishing out refreshments that he hadn't really been looking too hard. Becca came sauntering up to the table, dressed as a Southern belle, and leaned in close.

"I don't know what you think you're doing, Taylor. I saw you've signed up as a volunteer for all the events. Jackson is not and never will be interested in you. Let it go and stay away from us."

"Believe it or not, Becca, not everything is about you or your boyfriend. I'm working on making my life better and trying to get somewhere. Volunteer opportunities look good on college applications, so that's what I'm going to do. I'm awfully sorry you don't like it... wait, no, I'm really not. Step back and leave me alone," he dismissed her. Surprisingly, he was remarkably calm.

Becca glared at him for a few moments and then swirled on her heels and stomped away. Taylor smiled smugly at the victory. The rest of the dance, she would glare at him every so often but kept a wide berth. Taylor finally noticed Jackson, done up in a sleek black-and-red pirate's costume, as he headed toward the dance floor. Becca saw him and took off in his direction, arms outstretched. He gave her a quick hug and then started to walk again, but she grabbed him up and dragged him to the center of the floor as the DJ played a slow song. She put her hands on his hips, her cheek against his chest, and began swaying softly to the music. Jackson looked around a bit before he, too, began moving to the beat. As the two dancers turned, Taylor saw Becca look over at him, staring venomous daggers in his direction, and slide her hands down toward Jackson's butt. He knew the sick smile she gave him was meant to show him he hadn't won, he never would, and she would always be where Taylor himself could only dream of standing. He gazed at her, shrugged, and went back to serving drinks, as if his heart wasn't breaking just a little.

As the dance was winding down and the students started leaving for the night, Taylor noticed a dark-haired guy hanging around by the refreshment table. The guy seemed to be watching him, even though Taylor was sure he hadn't seen him before. It made him a little nervous. When the guy started approaching the table, Taylor turned and asked, "What can I get you?"

"Depends. Are you on the menu?" he leered.

"Uh… excuse me?" Taylor felt his face getting warm. He scrubbed fingers through his curly hair, looking around to see if anyone was listening.

"Oh, I'm sorry. I saw you looking at me. I thought maybe you were, you know, interested or something. I'm Kevin Richards," the stranger said, holding out his hand.

His grip was strong and warm. He didn't seem to want to let go of Taylor's hand, and Taylor found he didn't really mind. Kevin was nice-looking, about an inch or so taller than him, with pale blue eyes. The firefighter costume he wore stretched across his broad chest and legs, making him appear larger than he was. It was definitely a striking combination.

"Are you new here? I don't remember seeing you before," Taylor asked.

"No, I go to Milwaukee Tech," Kevin replied, his voice smooth. "I'm here with some friends. Do you know Mitch Daniels?"

"Yeah, he's on our baseball team."

"Right. I'm buddies with his brother. He told me there was a costume dance tonight, and it sounded like fun, so figured I'd come along. Glad I did, otherwise I might not have met you." Kevin grinned, looking Taylor up and down.

Taylor blushed hard. Kevin lowered his voice. "Look, I don't want to cause any issues. You know what I'm saying to you, right?"

Taylor nodded. "I think so."

"And?" he pressed, leaning on the table, a smirk spreading across his face.

Glancing back to the dance floor, he saw Becca still holding on to Jackson. Jackson glared at him. Taylor sighed. "Yeah, I might be interested," he said with a small smile.

"Cool. Here, lemme see your cell."

Taylor handed over his phone, and Kevin put his number into it. "Give me a call. Maybe we can get together, yeah? See what happens?"

"Sure, I think I'd like that," Taylor answered.

Suddenly the night looked just a little bit better.

THE first dance organized by Jackson's student council was a huge success. Quite a bit of money was raised, ensuring the council would be able to continue to make needed changes. They discussed more healthy options for meals in the cafeteria, including some vegetarian and vegan items; having some juniors and seniors visit the junior high school to talk about bullying; Arts Day, where senior citizens from the nearby center would come to the school and look at art projects done by the students; and collecting coats and blankets for the homeless shelters. There was a list of amazing ideas, and it seemed Jackson's attitude was infectious. People who were not normally joiners were getting into the spirit of the programs and really going all out to make them a success. It seemed weird. Jackson was taking a disparate group of people and bringing them together to improve the school and the community.

"Tay, I understand how you can love the guy. You were right last year. He seems so perfect. I just don't get what he sees in Becca," Benny said as he handed Taylor a soda.

Taylor sucked in a deep breath and then let it out slowly. "Maybe he sees a side of her we don't? Maybe she's not always a… well, maybe she's got some good points."

Benny reached out and grabbed Taylor's arm. "Who are you and what have you done with my best friend? I mean, you look like Taylor, but you seem so… I dunno, almost grown-up. It's kind of eerie."

"I think it's my friend who makes me this way," he replied with a hint of a smile. "I know he's having a good impact on my schoolwork."

"Are you really going to volunteer at everything this year?" Benny asked, the concern in his voice very obvious. "That seems like an awful lot, especially combined with your school load. If you really want to get your grades up, you may need to rethink that."

"I'm not going to fall into the same pit I did last year, I promise. If I find I can't handle it, I'll definitely bow out. I want to check out this chance, just like you. I really want to see what we can accomplish together."

Benny smiled at Taylor. "You don't know what it means to me that you want us to do this together," he said, his broad grin growing wider. "I always figured we'd end up drifting away from each other as we got older. I'd get married, and you'd be out slutting around, and we wouldn't really see each other except for maybe some holidays or something. I'd have kids, and you'd be out playing around, and then even the holidays wouldn't seem to happen. I was afraid to lose what we have."

"Slutting around?" Taylor sputtered. "I'll have you know that unlike *you,* I have standards. And so ya know, that speech would have been a lot better if you'd left out the lies about you getting married, because we both know ain't no one ever gonna put up with your crap."

For just a moment Benny looked shocked, and then both of them collapsed into peals of laughter. Taylor looked at Benny for a few moments, eyes brightening as he thought about his friend.

"You've always been the one to help others, Benny. You're the one who helped to make me who I am. We've always been more than friends. You're more like a companion, or a brother. My life isn't complete without you in it," Taylor said reverentially.

Benny was silent for a minute. Taylor thought he was digesting what he'd heard. "Is this the part where we kiss?" Benny asked with an amused grin.

"Ass."

"You want to kiss my ass? And here I thought you didn't know anything about romance!"

Taylor smiled, picked up his sketchpad, and started drawing a picture of his best friend. Strong, bold, confident. He shaded it so it appeared the light was coming from behind Benny. It was probably one of his most heartfelt works.

"Benny, I sorta met someone at the dance. He asked me out," Taylor mentioned, not looking up from the sketchpad.

"Holy crap! Really? Do tell. Name?" Benny asked incredulously.

"Kevin. He goes to school at Milwaukee Tech. He came up to me at the refreshment table, and I think he was hitting on me."

"You *think* he was hitting on you?"

Taylor crossed his arms and gave an exasperated sigh. "Well, it's not like I have a lot of experience in the matter."

"You gonna go out with him?" Benny was quiet for a moment. "What about Jax?"

Taylor sighed and carded his hand through his hair. "He was with Becca last night, and I know nothing is going to happen between us. Maybe if I finally move on, I can find a way to just be friends with him."

"That could work. It might help you out too. Get you a bit of social action, if you know what I'm talking about," Benny said, waggling his eyebrows.

Taylor grinned and rolled his eyes. "God, I just met this guy, and you've already got me in bed with him. You're a fast worker. Is that what it was with you and Sheila?"

"You know me, buddy—strike while the iron is hot! This might be *your* only chance to not die a virgin," Benny snickered. "Besides, Sheila was totally into me. Who could blame her?"

"You suck."

"You wish!"

"I gotta get home." Taylor laughed. "Thanks for helping me tonight."

He finished the picture and handed it to Benny, then said "thank you" before grabbing his backpack and heading out into the early evening.

TAYLOR called Kevin a few days later. They talked for a while, getting to know a little about each other. Kevin, it turned out, was a senior at Milwaukee Tech. He had sent applications for several colleges in California, wanting to get away from Milwaukee's winter weather. He planned on becoming an architect, wanted a family, enjoyed working around the yard. Taylor enjoyed listening to his plans. Kevin definitely sounded like he had an outline for his life.

"So what are you doing this weekend, Taylor?" Kevin asked, his voice rich and full.

"Just some studying, but don't really have anything planned," Taylor replied, flexing his fingers nervously.

"I was thinking about heading over to the museum. Haven't been there in a while, and there's a couple new exhibits I wanted to check out. Think you might want to come with?"

"Oh God, I haven't been there since I was, like, ten. Do they still have that creepy old woman in the rocking chair?"

"Yeah, I think she's on the Streets of Old Milwaukee. She creeped you out too?"

"So much. When I was a kid, I thought she lived there or something. Yeah, I'd like to go. I can meet you there at ten o'clock?"

"Nah, I'll pick you up, if that's cool?"

"Yeah, I'd like that," Taylor answered brightly, his nervousness dissipating.

They firmed up their plans, talked for a while longer, and then Taylor reluctantly told Kevin he had to finish his homework.

"Not a problem, babe, I'll see you Saturday," Kevin replied and disconnected.

It took Taylor a minute to get over the shock of being called "babe" by anyone. He kind of liked the feeling. Suddenly Saturday couldn't come quickly enough.

PITCH

CHAPTER SIX

ON DATING AND OTHER THINGS

THANKS to Benny's tutoring, Taylor's grades showed a marked improvement. Where before he had been a B- student, he now moved into the B+ range and even flirted with A- on occasion. Even with the extra work he did volunteering, he was able to keep his promise to Benny and made sure his schoolwork came first. His teachers were very pleased with his progress and mentioned it to him often. He thanked them, but then made sure to tell them Benny was the one who'd been helping him. The teachers were quite impressed with the success and asked Benny if he would be willing to tutor some other students. Benny was on top of the world, even if it meant less free time for him.

Promptly at 10:00 a.m. on Saturday, Kevin rang Taylor's doorbell. When he answered he found the young man standing outside, a single yellow rose clutched in his hand. Kevin smiled and held it out to Taylor. Taylor blushed hard and accepted the flower.

"The lady at the florist told me a yellow rose signifies joy, gladness, friendship, delight, promise of a new beginning, and says 'remember me'. I figure all of those things are important and really wanted you to have it."

"It's pretty," Taylor said, taking a light sniff.

"Not half as pretty as you, babe," Kevin said, grinning. "You ready to go?"

"Yeah, I'm ready. Thanks for picking me up."

Kevin waggled his eyebrows. "That's what I was trying to do at the dance. Glad to see it worked."

Taylor laughed. He found Kevin charming and funny and, okay, fine, a little sexy.

The museum was pretty crowded, with people gathering to admire the Cleopatra exhibit on loan from Egypt. Kevin led Taylor by the hand to several exhibits, stopping at them long enough to give Taylor a bit of information about each one. As they rounded the corner in a darkened area, Kevin leaned over, gave Taylor a quick kiss, and squeezed his hand. Then it was off to the next exhibit. They ran around for hours, checking out the newer areas, visiting the Cleopatra display and being completely captivated by it, and sneaking kisses whenever they had the opportunity. Taylor noticed Kevin seemed to enjoy touching him, holding hands, touching his shoulder, rubbing against him. He was really enjoying the attention. After a quick lunch, they decided to head out.

"Oh God, that was fun," Taylor said, laughing. "That old lady in the rocking chair? She's still just as creepy as ever." He cringed jokingly.

"I know, right! Thanks for coming with me, Taylor. I'm having a great time."

"Same. I'm really enjoying being here with you," he said as they got into the car.

Kevin put his hand on Taylor's leg, leaned over, and kissed him hard. Taylor opened his mouth to the kiss and noticed Kevin tasted of peppermint.

"Why don't you come over to my house?" Kevin asked. "We can watch a movie or something."

"Yeah, I'd like that."

When they arrived at Kevin's house, Taylor was damn impressed. The house was a large colonial style, with white siding and black trim, surrounded by an expertly manicured lawn. As they entered the foyer, Taylor gawked at the salmon-colored walls adorned with exquisite landscape paintings he thought he could just lose himself in. He looked at them closely and was surprised to see that they were all original artworks, not reproductions. They must have cost a fortune to collect. He was completely immersed in them when Kevin shut the door and stepped closer to him.

"You smell nice," he said, bringing his mouth near Taylor's ear. He flicked his tongue out just enough to lick the lobe. Taylor shivered.

"Liked that, did ya?" Kevin said with obvious delight. He pressed in closer, nibbling on Taylor's neck. "Why don't you come up to my room?" he asked, grabbing Taylor by the hand, encouraging him to follow Kevin up the large staircase.

"Holy crap, this is your room?"

Taylor looked around. A large four-poster bed, covered with a dark blue comforter, dominated the center of the room; an entertainment center with a flat-screen television stood against the wall nearby. A cherry desk, complete with an Apple computer, was set flush against the far wall. Everything was so clean and well organized Taylor just had to mention it.

"Yeah, it's okay. We've got a maid who keeps everything nice and neat," Kevin said. "C'mere."

Kevin pulled Taylor against his body, moving his mouth over Taylor's. Kevin ran his hands across Taylor's back, moving up and down, brushing against his ass. Taylor closed his eyes and melted into the kiss. His stomach fluttered. He couldn't believe how nervous he was. He'd thought about being kissed so many times, but now that it was actually happening, he wasn't sure what to do with himself. When Kevin put his hands on Taylor's face, pulling him deeper into the kiss, Taylor groaned as Kevin's tongue flicked against his lips. Taylor shivered when Kevin sucked at his tongue. Breaking away, Kevin started nipping at Taylor's neck, pressing his obvious erection into Taylor's leg. He grabbed Taylor's ass and began massaging the cheeks.

Taylor stiffened and pulled back. "What are you doing?"

"Oh come on, you know you want it too," he said with a leer.

Taylor took a few steps back, holding up his hands. "Kevin, I'm not really comfortable with this. I don't want to do this."

"Yeah, you do. Stop playing around," he said, grabbing at Taylor's arm, digging his nails into the soft flesh.

"Look, I said no," Taylor nearly shouted, yanking his arm away. "I think this might not have been a very good idea. I'm gonna go ahead and go home. I'll talk to you later, okay?"

Kevin glared at him, fury in his eyes. "You're a fucking tease, Taylor. You can't be turning me on all day, then come here and say no."

Heat flashed through Taylor's body. He gave Kevin an icy stare and snapped, "I didn't do anything to turn you on. You know what? Whatever, I'm out of here."

Taylor took a step toward the door. He didn't even notice the fist coming at his face until it slammed into his eye. He fell back onto the floor, writhing in pain.

"You're a bitch, Taylor! Fucking tease!" Kevin screamed, kicking Taylor in the ribs.

Taylor tried to scramble away. His ribs hurt like they were on fire. Kevin made a grab for him, but Taylor pushed him back, causing Kevin to fall to the floor and giving Taylor the chance to get to his feet. He staggered to the stairs, his breath ragged. God it hurt to breathe. He stumbled through the foyer and out the door. He tried to run from the house but could only limp along. His side and face were throbbing, his eye hurt, and he was humiliated. He could hear Kevin screaming his name, but he refused to stop. After he'd gotten several blocks from the house, he took out his cell and called Benny.

"Tay, how's the date?"

"Worst date ever. Can you come get me?" he pleaded.

"I'm in the middle of a tutoring session. Can you give me a bit?"

Taylor started sobbing into the phone. "Benny, please. I really need you. Please?"

"Taylor? What's wrong? Where are you?'

Taylor began gulping air. His skin was clammy, and his heart raced. He tried to concentrate on his breathing but couldn't focus.

"Taylor!" Benny yelled sharply. "Where the hell are you?"

Taylor tried to answer but couldn't speak. He dropped his phone, curled up on the grass, and sobbed. He wasn't sure how long he lay there before he felt strong arms surrounding him, rubbing his back. He lurched up and began to flail, trying to escape from the grip, only to stop when he looked up and saw Benny's face.

"Oh God, Tay, what happened? What happened to your face?" Benny asked, looking at the large bruises that were no doubt beginning to form around Taylor's eye. He gently ran his fingers over the affected area, stopping when Taylor flinched.

Taylor turned and pressed his face into Benny's chest and sobbed harshly. Benny said nothing else, just held on, stroking his head.

"It'll be okay, Taylor. I promise you're going to be all right. Just let it out. I'm here. I've got you," Benny whispered softly to him.

When Taylor finally calmed down enough to speak, he told Benny what had happened.

"I'll kill that son of a bitch, Tay. I swear to God he's a dead man," Benny snarled, his hands clenched tightly at his sides.

Taylor saw the rage on Benny's face and shrank away from him. "Benny, no, please. Just take me home."

The anger drained from Benny's face. He tucked Taylor tightly to his body, and his voice broke when he said, "I really think you need to go to the hospital. Let them X-ray your ribs and check out your eye. It's all bloodshot." Benny reached out and traced the corner of Taylor's eye.

"All I want is to go home and lay down. It doesn't hurt much anymore, really," Taylor replied wearily.

Benny helped Taylor to his feet, put his arms around him, and started moving him toward the car.

"How'd you find me, Benny?" Taylor asked as Benny practically carried him to the car.

Benny flushed. Taylor could tell his friend was nervous. "I… look, Tay, I had to call your folks. I told them I thought you were in trouble, and you called me for help. They used an app on the phone to find out where you were. I'm sorry, I couldn't think of anything else to do."

"S'okay, Benny. Thanks for coming to get me. I'm sorry I interrupted your tutor session," Taylor said, tears once again forming in his eyes.

"Shut up, man. You're one of the most important things in my life." Benny's voice turned angry once again. "I swear I'm gonna pound him. He never shoulda put his hands on you."

"Just let it go, Benny. Promise me you'll let it go?" Taylor pleaded.

"No, I'm not letting it go. I'm gonna kill him," Benny declared, his voice hard and strained. Taylor hadn't heard that tone since Benny had talked about Addy's father.

"Benny, please. I really just want to forget this happened. I need you to let it go. I'm begging you, Benny, please don't do anything. I don't want you to get in trouble."

Benny sighed as he opened the door and put Taylor into the car.

"This isn't a good answer. We really should call the cops. He assaulted you! What's to stop him from doing it to anyone else?" Benny spat out.

"I just can't, Benny. I can't deal with this."

"Look, man, I don't think it's a good idea. He hurt you, and he could hurt someone else, but I can't force you to do this. I won't touch him, but you need to think this through."

Taylor slumped against the seat. He doubted Benny was going to let it go, but he was glad his friend wasn't going to act on his anger against Kevin. He'd think about what Benny said, but right now he just didn't have the energy. He rested his head against the window, silent, trying not to think about Kevin until Benny got him home.

"Oh God, Taylor, what happened?" his mother asked as she rushed to the car.

"It's okay, Mom. I'm okay."

Benny took charge of the situation. "Mrs. Andrews, I'm going to put Taylor in his bed, okay? He needs some rest. Can you get him an icepack or something for his eye?"

"But what happened to him? What's going on?"

Benny turned toward Mrs. Andrews. "We can talk about this later, okay? Taylor needs to lie down. Can you please just get him an icepack for his eye?" he asked. Taylor saw Benny scowl and could tell his friend was trying to stifle his anger.

Taylor's mom hesitated for a moment.

"Honest, Mom," Taylor promised, "I'm fine."

"Mrs. Andrews, can we talk about this after I get him upstairs?" Benny pleaded.

Mrs. Andrews looked at her son, then to Benny. "Sure, I'll meet you both upstairs."

Benny helped Taylor up the stairs and laid him on the bed. "Look, you need to tell her. She's worried."

"I know. I was going to do it when she came upstairs. It's not how I pictured it going, but I need to let her know," Taylor said, resigned to the conversation.

His mom stepped into the room a few moments later.

"Mom, can you sit down a sec? I need to talk to you." He waited as his mom sat near him. Benny moved toward the door. "Benny, would you stay? Please?" Taylor asked.

"Are you sure you want me to?" Benny replied, glancing over to Taylor.

"Yeah, Benny, it's cool. Please stay." Taylor's gazed darted from his best friend to his mother. He closed his eyes and said the words he'd been hiding for so many years. "Mom, I'm gay."

For a moment silence reigned. Then he heard his mom sniffle. The mattress moved when she sat, slid over, and took him into her arms.

66

"Oh, baby, thank you for telling me. You don't know how glad I am you finally trusted me."

"You... knew?"

"Yes, Taylor, your dad and I figured it out a while ago, but we wanted you to be the one to tell us. I know how hard it must have been, but I'm so grateful you told me. Now, please tell me what happened today."

Taylor sighed and recounted the story to his mother. She was nearly as angry as Benny.

"Mom, I don't want to deal with this, please. I just want to let it go."

"Taylor Aaron Andrews, you listen to me," his mother said sharply. "If you let him get away with this, the next person might not be so lucky. What do you think will happen if you find out he seriously hurt someone? How do you think that'll make you feel?"

"Mom, it's going to be my word against his. From the looks of his house, his folks have money. And what do I say? He hit me? That's hardly going to be a crime. Kids have fights all the time."

His mother glared at him but slumped her shoulders when she saw how adamant he was. "Taylor, this is a bad idea, but I can't make you do anything if you don't want to."

THAT evening at dinner they told Taylor's father everything. He reacted pretty much the same as everyone else: angry, frustrated. He took Taylor's phone and dialed Kevin's number, despite Taylor's pleading. His voice was harsh as he lit into whoever was on the other end of the phone. When he hung up, his face was flushed with anger.

"Dad, what's the matter?"

"That little son of a bitch laughed and hung up on me," he growled.

"Dad, I'm letting it go. I don't want to face him. I don't want to deal with him."

"Taylor, I know you're upset. I know he hurt you. I understand your feelings, and I'll respect your wishes, but I hate that he's going to get away with this."

"I'm sorry, Dad, I just can't face him. I thought he liked me, really. I thought I could like him, but I didn't want him. He's not the one I—" Taylor stopped when he realized what he was about to say.

Taylor turned away from his family, his eyes filling with tears. Benny pulled up a chair and sat down beside him and began rubbing Taylor's back, something he'd often done to help Taylor calm down.

"Mom, Dad, can I talk to Benny alone, please?"

"Sure, Taylor. We'll be in the living room if you need us, okay?" his mother replied.

Taylor nodded. His parents stood and made their way into the other room.

"He's not the one, Benny," Taylor said softly. "When Kevin started to touch me, I tried to think about him. But when he started grinding against me, I got scared. He's not the one I wanted, and I wasn't ready to give him what he was asking for."

"You listen to me, Taylor. He wasn't *asking* you for something. He was trying to take it from you. I know I made a joke out of it the other day, but you shouldn't ever do something just because. You made the right choice, Tay, I swear. I'm just sorry you got hurt."

Benny gathered him up in his arms again, pulled back, and inspected his bruised face. "You're gonna look like crap in the morning. It's a good thing you're more than just another pretty face," Benny said, trying to force a smile.

Taylor studied Benny. He could see the muscles in Benny's jaw tighten like he could barely contain himself. "Benny, remember your promise. Just let it go," Taylor said quietly.

Benny gave a curt nod. "Are you going to be okay, Taylor? I have to work up a lesson plan tonight and really should get going."

"Yeah, Benny. Thank you for today. I didn't know who else to call."

Benny grabbed his shoulders and peered into his eyes. "You will always call me, Tay. We're going to be there for each other, right?" Benny said, pulling Taylor into a quick hug.

"Yeah," Taylor said, sniffling. "You know we are."

Benny grabbed his keys and headed out the door. Taylor walked into the living room and found his parents in animated conversation. When they saw him, they stopped talking.

"You guys know I'm seventeen now, right?" he asked.

His parents regarded him curiously.

"When I was a kid and you guys had an argument, you'd always stop talking when I walked in. I kinda know you're doing it again," he said, chuckling.

"We're not arguing, Taylor," his father started and ran his fingers through his hair. "We're trying to understand the situation. What did you mean when you said this boy wasn't the one? Is there someone else?"

Taylor sighed. He really didn't want to talk about this with his parents. All he wanted to do was go upstairs and climb under the blankets and just forget this whole mess. "Jackson Kern," he finally said. "He's the pitcher on our baseball team. I've liked him since the moment I saw him, but he's going out with Becca Monroe, the cheerleader from school."

"So he's not gay? Taylor, this Kevin hurt you physically," his mother said, with obvious disgust. "Obsessing over a straight guy is going to hurt you emotionally."

"You think I haven't thought of that, Mom?" Taylor said, agitated. "You think I don't realize how much it hurts? When I tried to talk to him, I found out he thinks I'm disgusting. Yet I can't help the way I feel. I try not to like him, but it just doesn't work out like that. I see him, you know? He's so confident. He's so willing to put others ahead of himself. It's like he's so damn noble, but somehow the thought of me disgusts him. I don't get it. It's like he's two completely different people… and, yeah, it hurts, Mom."

He turned and ran up to his room, slammed the door, and threw himself on the bed. After a few minutes, he heard a hesitant knock.

"Taylor? Can I come in?"

"Sure, Mom," he said with a sniffle.

The door opened and his mother strode across the floor, sat on the bed, and pulled him into a hug. "Honey, I'm sorry. We didn't mean to upset you. We're not really sure how to be there for you."

"You are, Mom, believe me. I was really surprised when you told me you knew I was gay, and I'm so glad you're okay about it. Becca knows, too, I think. And I think she would try to use it against me if she thought I would try to get between her and Jackson." Taylor gave a slight shiver at the thought. "I was afraid to tell you, but I was more afraid of you finding out from someone else and being upset or disappointed in me."

"Oh, Taylor, you're too damn emotional for your own good," she said with a sniff.

"Yeah," Taylor laughed, "can't imagine where that comes from."

"Taylor, please listen to me carefully. I need you to hear these words because they're very, very important. Your father and I love you. We always have. We always will. Gay or straight, you will always be our son, and we will always be proud of you," she said emphatically. "Don't let others choose the kind of person you're going to be. Don't let this Becca girl use something like this against you. You have always been there for everyone else. Stand up and be proud of *yourself* for a change. Take that power away from her."

She kissed him on the head and left the room, quietly closing the door behind her. Taylor lay back on the bed and pondered her words for a while until he fell asleep.

MONDAY morning he entered the school and hurried to homeroom. His face still ached. The bruises had deepened and turned darker.

His eye was swollen and black. He could feel everyone staring at him. He sat down at his desk and groaned when Becca noticed him. She laughed with her friends for a few minutes and turned toward him, smiling brightly. She jumped up and rushed over to his desk.

"Oh my goodness, Taylor, what happened?" she asked with mock sincerity.

"Go away, Becca. Leave me alone," Taylor growled.

"That really looks like it hurts," she chuckled. "Jackson had an early meeting with the student council, and I can't wait for him to get here so he can see—"

Jackson entered the room and put his books on his desk. He turned, his eyes locked on Taylor. He frowned, his face set in a harsh squint, and stepped toward Taylor, only to be blocked by Becca. He brushed her aside and stopped at Taylor's desk.

"Taylor? What happened to your face?" he asked, his expression an unreadable mask.

"Nothing. Why won't you just leave me alone?" Taylor snapped.

Becca took Jackson by the arm and tried to pull him away, but he shrugged her off. "Taylor, can we talk?" he asked quietly.

The bell rang, and the other students moved to the door, intent on heading to their first period class. Taylor stood up, gathered his books, and glared at Jackson.

"Yeah, I think it's pretty clear that's not going to happen, and we both know it, don't we?" he shot back. Turning on his heel, he rushed out the door, not even pausing when he heard Jackson call his name.

CHAPTER SEVEN
OUT AND ABOUT

THE day had been hell. People he didn't even know kept asking him what happened, kept asking questions he didn't feel like answering, kept badgering him with their stupidity. He was grateful when it was over and he could go home. Just as he was about to go through the door, he heard his name being called. He stopped and found Mitch Daniels approaching him.

"Dude, what the hell? Why would you think it's okay to do that kind of shit?"

Taylor blinked a couple times, trying to comprehend what Mitch was talking about. He waited a few seconds, figuring Mitch would finally finish his thought, but decided the shortstop was expecting him to reply.

"What are you talking about, Mitch?" Taylor finally asked.

"I heard what happened with Kevin. What were you thinking? Why would you be touching on him and trying to get up on him?"

Taylor gasped. His stomach started to churn, the bile rising into his throat. His breathing grew sharper. Mitch stood there, glaring at him. Taylor's hands were sweating now.

"Who said that, Mitch? Who have you been talking to?"

"Kevin told Cody what you did, man. That's seriously messed up. It's no wonder he had to beat you down. You don't go trying to touch some dude's junk, man. That's all kinds of wrong. I mean, I don't care if you're… you know, that way, but man you can't be doing that to other guys," he spat.

Taylor's world began spinning. He swallowed hard, resisting the urge to heave. He was trapped. He couldn't breathe. Everything was fuzzy. He heard voices that seemed so far away. He felt something touch him, and then suddenly he didn't feel anything at all.

"MR. ANDREWS?"

Taylor heard a voice calling from far away. It was a calm voice, so soothing. He was warm and comfortable. He opened his eyes a crack. He'd never noticed the pattern on the floor before, not really. Kind of a mosaic tile in different shades of brown and white. It really was kind of pretty.

"Mr. Andrews?"

The voice again. This time more insistent. A hand touched him on the shoulder, shaking him gently. Suddenly everything came back with blinding intensity. Kevin had said Taylor tried to touch him. That Taylor was responsible for his own beating. He struggled to sit upright, caught under the watchful eye of Mr. Dean and a few students. He saw Mitch there, glaring down at him.

"Mr. Andrews, are you okay? There's an ambulance on the way. Just lie back down."

"M'okay," Taylor mumbled. He tried forcing himself to a standing position, but the effort was too much. Mr. Dean put his hand on Taylor's arm and eased him back down.

"I'm pretty sure you need to stay where you are, Mr. Andrews. Can't have you getting hurt on school property," he chuckled, trying to smile. Taylor decided he should do it more often. It was kind of a nice smile.

The paramedics strapped Taylor to a gurney. They did a preliminary check, asking him to count to ten, asking who the president was, asking if he knew his name and where he was. He answered all the questions correctly, but he started to get agitated when they asked him if he could remember what happened. He was angry. He wanted to run but couldn't move. They kept asking him what he remembered, and he could feel the panic bubbling again. He didn't want to talk, and he didn't want to think about the fact that the whole school was laughing at him. He squeezed his eyes tight, wishing it would all just go away. He felt his world slipping into darkness again.

TAYLOR shivered involuntarily from the cold against his chest. He opened his eyes and tried to focus on the person, a woman, maybe, hovering over him.

"I know it's cold, Taylor, I'm sorry. I'll be done in just a minute or two. I'm Dr. Kovac, and I'm just checking your vital signs. You had us worried for a bit. If your friend hadn't caught you, well, let's just say you'd probably have a lot more than a black eye," she said with a smile.

Taylor tried to say something, wanted to ask who caught him, but couldn't get his mouth to work.

"We've given you a pretty strong sedative, Taylor. Your mom is here, and we let her know that we'll be keeping you, at least overnight, just to make sure everything is going the way it should. She says you've been under a lot of stress, and I think you'll need to rest a couple of days. You've got some pretty deep bruising on your ribs. We did some X-rays, but there doesn't appear to be anything broken. They're going to be tender for a while, but I don't think there's anything else we need to do about them," the doctor said, then lowered her voice to barely a whisper. "Your mom, she's pretty worried, so just rest up and let her baby you, okay?"

He tried to roll his eyes, but all they did was close.

TAYLOR heard someone speaking near his ear. The voice was deep and smooth. He couldn't really make out most of the words, but he thought someone was touching his hand. He tried to open his eyes, to see who was in the room with him, but he just couldn't seem to make them respond. Before he tumbled back to sleep, he thought he heard "sorry" and "take care of it," and then something brushed his cheek. Warmth wrapped around his chest and then nothing.

"Benny?" he mumbled.

It was dark outside when Taylor opened his eyes. He could see a crescent moon hovering just over the roof of the hospital. His cell phone was on the nightstand. He reached out and pushed the button. It was 8:43. He called Benny's number but got no answer. After leaving a short message, which he wasn't even certain was in English, Taylor disconnected. He got up and stumbled toward the bathroom, grateful that they seemed to have removed the IV. He was lightheaded but really had to pee. Standing was out of the question, so he sat down on the toilet, his head lolling from side to side. He'd never been this out of it before. Thoughts tried to form in his head, but they were terribly disjointed. After flushing the toilet, he trudged back to the bed, lay down, and was quickly asleep.

"Good morning, Taylor," the nurse called out.

Taylor's eyes cracked open. Light was streaming into his room. He grumbled and buried his face into the pillow.

"Come on, get up. I need to check to see how you're doing. Are you hungry?" She reached behind the bed and pulled out a menu. "This is our room service menu. Take a look, see if there's something that interests you, and we'll get you some breakfast."

Taylor mumbled, "Thank you." His stomach wasn't settling well, so he decided not to eat.

She quickly checked his blood pressure and pulse. "Are there any questions you have?" She smiled when he shook his head. "The doctor will be in to see you later. Have a good day."

He went to the bathroom again, still lightheaded, but not as bad as he had been the night before. He was ambling back to the bed when the door opened and a quiet voice echoed inside the room.

"Tay?"

"Benny?"

His friend entered, leaving the door ajar, and moved over to the side of the bed. Taylor was trying to figure out how to get back in the bed when he heard Benny chuckle. Taking Taylor by the arm, he guided him back onto the narrow mattress and covered him with the thin blanket.

"Thank you," Taylor mumbled. He squinted at Benny's face, seeing the worry reflected there. "Shouldn't you be in school?" Taylor asked.

"Tay... I heard... uh...."

Taylor let out a sigh. "Yeah, Benny, I know what you heard. I guess Kevin got the last laugh after all, huh?"

"Well, no. Look, maybe I should just talk to you about this later. You don't look like you're even going to remember me being here." Benny laughed weakly.

"Tell me, Benny. What happened?"

Benny ran his fingers through his stubbly hair. "Look, Tay... someone beat Kevin up. They broke his nose, blackened his eye, his face is a serious mess. His folks called the cops. He wouldn't tell them who did it, but he told them he had hit you and that he lied about why. He told them what he did, Tay."

"Benny, you didn't...?"

Benny's eyes darkened as he glared at Taylor. "No, Taylor, I didn't!" Benny spat out indignantly. "I told you I wouldn't. Do you really think that little of me? Do you really think I'd break my promise to you?"

Taylor struggled to say something. Benny stared at him in silence for a few moments, and then he spun on his heel and left the room without another word, leaving Taylor alone and with the distinct feeling he'd just lost his best friend in the whole world.

TAYLOR'S mom brought him home early Wednesday afternoon. The doctor told them Taylor was suffering from exhaustion, not uncommon considering his workload and volunteering. She recommended he take the rest of the week off from school and stay in bed, reminding them that a high level of stress could trigger another panic attack.

Once he was settled in bed, Taylor had tried to reach Benny, hoping to apologize, but his call went to voice mail. He left a message, asking him to please call back. Taylor stared at the phone, desperately wanting it to ring. Wanting Benny to tell him everything would be okay again. When it didn't his shoulders slumped, and he slid the phone into his pocket again.

"Taylor?" his mom asked, coming into his room. "Are you hungry?"

Taylor gave a small start. His stomach rumbled. He hadn't really eaten since school on Monday, but he'd been so tired he couldn't even think of food, and the blowup with Benny on Tuesday didn't help. Taylor couldn't remember the last time he'd gone a full day without talking to his friend, and it was eating him up. "No, Mom, not really. Thanks anyway."

"You need to eat something, Taylor. I'm going to bring up a sandwich, and you try to eat, okay?"

Taylor just nodded and lay back on the bed. He sank into the pillows, trying to fight sleep, but this was way more comfortable than the hospital bed, and he quickly went under.

"*You know you wanted it, Taylor,*" Kevin sneered. "*You were practically begging for it.*"

A fist flew at his face again and again. At times it was Kevin. Then Benny. Then Jackson. They each took turns hitting him, pummeling his face: Kevin telling him what a failure he'd been as a lover, Benny saying he'd failed as a friend, and Jackson saying he was a waste of space as a person.

Taylor gasped sharply and sat up, curling the blankets around himself like they could protect him.

"Bad dream?"

He glanced over and saw Benny sitting in the chair beside his bed. For just an instant, he hesitated, thinking he was still dreaming and waiting for a fist to smack flesh.

"Tay? You okay?" Benny asked, obviously concerned, but he didn't move from the chair.

"Benny? You're really here?" He wouldn't take his eyes off his best friend. He couldn't chance him disappearing.

Benny gave a small chuckle. "Yeah, I'm really here. You okay? Do I need to get your mom?"

Relief flooded him. "God, Benny, I'm so sorry, I didn't mean to accuse you of anything, I swear I should have never said it and I was afraid you hated me and I'm so sorry…." The words flew out of his mouth in one long sentence.

Benny rubbed his hands over his face. "Look, I gotta be honest, I was hurt and overreacted. Thing is, though, I thought about it, Taylor. I really, really thought about breaking my word to you. I wanted him to understand he can't touch you. I wanted to be the one that did it, to protect you. They were talking in school about it, and I wanted to just do something. It seems like everyone heard *you* did something, but it doesn't seem like many cared *he* admitted to lying."

Taylor knew how much his friend hated Kevin, but in that moment all he could see was Benny's concern for Taylor's safety. It warmed him to know his friend cared so much.

"It's not gonna be easy to go back to school, you know," Benny added.

Taylor gave him a resigned smile. "I already figured that out, Benny. When Mitch told me Kevin sold that line of crap to his brother, I knew what was gonna happen. My mom told me the police came by, asking about Kevin's story. My folks told them I had no interest in pressing charges. I don't know how it's going to go at school, though." He dropped his gaze and stared at the floor. He'd heard the horror stories of people coming out in high school. He knew how people were going to act toward him. He shivered as he thought about what was to come.

"What are we gonna do about it?" Benny asked curiously. Taylor raised his eyes and stared at Benny. He could see the concerned expression on Benny's face. Taylor knew he couldn't let Benny get caught up in what was going to happen.

"Well, *we* aren't going to do anything. I don't want you tarred with the same brush as me, so I'll understand if you need to step away from it."

Benny's face drained and then flashed crimson. "You are such a freaking idiot, Taylor!" he roared. "I know you've been my best friend for twelve years, but God, sometimes you can be so stupid. Do you get that?" He threw his hands in the air and stalked around the room. "Twelve years, Taylor. Almost my whole life. From pee pants to now, I have always stood by you. Do you really think I'd push you aside? Do you honestly believe I give a rat's ass about what people say about me?"

Taylor could hear the anger in the words and see the pain creasing his friend's face. "I just wanted to give you an out, Benny. I don't want you hurt because of me," Taylor said meekly.

"Seriously?" Benny snapped. "What you're doing now will hurt me a lot more than what anyone else does. Please don't try to push me away. Besides, you're not really good at the whole noble thing. That's *my* gig."

Benny gave a small smile that still lit his whole face, and he rushed over to Taylor, pulling him into a firm but gentle hug. "We're going to get through this. But we're gonna do it together, just like we've done our whole lives. Do you understand me?" Benny mumbled into his shoulder.

Taylor nodded numbly. He didn't trust himself to speak because he knew he'd burst into tears and probably wouldn't be able to stop.

TAYLOR'S return to school was surprisingly unremarkable. Mitch Daniels apologized to him and admitted he'd been the one to catch Taylor as he fell, for which Taylor was grateful. There were a few comments, but nothing like the open hostility he had feared. People stared, but he wasn't sure if it was because of the fading bruises on his face or the stories they'd heard. By and large, most people just ignored him as usual. Unfortunately, not all of them did.

"Welcome back, Taylor. We were so worried about you," Becca said with a snotty arrogance.

"I'm sure you were, Becca. You always have everyone's best interest at heart," Taylor returned with a hard stare.

He took his seat and groaned inwardly as she followed him. When she got close enough, she leaned forward and whispered to him, "Jax and I found the whole thing to be pretty damn funny. We had a good laugh about it. God, I can't believe you would actually think some guy would be interested in you for anything other than maybe a pity hookup."

Taylor blanched. He closed his eyes and started concentrating on his breathing. In. Out. In. Out.

"Do you want to know what Jax said, Taylor? He said even if you didn't start it, you probably still deserved it. He just couldn't imagine anyone actually going through with touching you, even if it was to hit you." She chuckled darkly.

In. Out. In. Out. When he didn't react, she sniffed, and he could hear her heels as she stomped away. In. Out. In. Out.

When the bell rang he opened his eyes so he could gather his stuff. Jackson was looking at him, a look of pain etched across his face. Taylor sighed and headed out to first period.

"Why did the fag cross the road?" someone asked as he passed.

"To get to the dicks on the other side, of course!" came the reply.

In. Out. In. Out.

TWO weeks prior to Thanksgiving break, the student council announced a food drive. Due to Taylor's issues the previous couple of weeks, his parents weren't letting him help too much with it. He was able to collect some canned goods from the neighbors, though, and had Benny help him deliver them to the school. The students took in hundreds of cans and boxes of food, which they then donated to the local food banks. The *Milwaukee Journal-Sentinel* did a story on the amazing student council and their president reaching out to help the community. Jackson explained there had been some students in his former school who were in trouble when their father lost his job. They had very little money and could barely put together enough food for the family. They'd come to school hungry many times, but the community rallied around them and ensured they would have something to eat. Jackson wanted the school to adopt the same principles, looking out for each other and making sure no one should suffer because they couldn't afford food.

Yet another feather in Jackson's cap.

By the time Thanksgiving rolled around, Taylor was pretty much yesterday's news. He still heard stuff from people, mostly behind his back, but there weren't as many overt comments. True to his word, Benny had stood up for him whenever someone got in his face, like Larry Dykstra.

"So, I hear you're the school fag, huh?" Larry mocked.

Taylor stood quietly, figuring if he ignored Larry he'd just go away. Larry didn't.

"I asked you a question, queer-boy. Don't you know you should always answer your betters?"

"He doesn't have any betters, Larry. Back off." Taylor had never been so happy to hear Benny's voice.

"Or what, Peters? Oh, are you his boyfriend?"

"No, asswipe, I'm his *best* friend. You have a problem with him, you're going to have a problem with me too."

Taylor smiled, feeling a bit stronger knowing Benny was there.

"Yes, Larry, I'm gay. No, I don't want to touch you. No, I don't think you're cute. No, I don't want to check you out in the shower. Was there anything else?" Taylor huffed with an exaggerated sigh.

Larry glared for a moment, then grumbled and stomped away, muttering something about what's wrong with him, not being good enough to be checked out in the showers. It cracked Benny up.

IT WAS the start of Thanksgiving break when Benny gave Taylor the bad news. "Tay," Benny began, "my parents told me I can't hang out with you anymore."

Taylor's entire world fell away. He knew the reason and it hurt. "It's because I'm gay, isn't it?" he said softly, his heart breaking at the thought of people he'd known his whole life rejecting him this way.

"Yeah, it is."

"M'sorry, Benny. I didn't mean to cause you any problems," Taylor mumbled, staring hard at the ground that he was wishing would just open up and swallow him.

Benny lifted Taylor's chin and stared into his eyes. "Tay, I told them you're my best friend and nothing would change that. They're not upset you're gay. They figure I'm going to lose focus on my schoolwork if I'm caught up in a big gay controversy."

"I don't understand?"

Benny crossed his arms over his broad chest. "I told them my friend comes first, last, and always." He smiled brightly. "I explained to them, very rationally I might add, if they said I couldn't hang out with you, my schoolwork really would suffer, and did they want to be responsible for that?"

Taylor laughed. Leave it to Benny to turn it back on his parents.

"So, my folks are going to visit the grands this week," Benny said, referring to his grandparents. "They said I could stay home, if you think your folks would be okay with me having Thanksgiving dinner here with you? I don't want to be an inconvenience."

"I think they'd be pretty upset if you didn't. You know how my folks feel about you," Taylor laughed.

"Yeah, but they still let me come over anyway!" Benny giggled.

Dinner was a veritable feast. Taylor knew his mom made certain she had plenty of vegan dishes for Benny, whose face lit up when he saw the work she'd put into it. They enjoyed the meal, then retired to the living room to play a rousing game of Scrabble. No one was surprised when Benny won. He was just too smart for his own good. When you know words like "gjetost," which Benny proved was a word—some kind of dark-brown Norwegian cheese, made primarily from goat's milk—your chances of winning are pretty high. Then Benny wondered why no one wanted to play with him.

WILL PARKINSON

CHAPTER EIGHT
GIFTED

HELPING the Homeless was Jackson's brainchild for the winter months. The students and faculty gathered lightly worn outerwear for kids and adults, as well as blankets and comforters, for the local homeless shelters. Taylor was thrilled about this project. So many people would be helped if they could get the local businesses involved. He asked several stores if they could help out, but managed only to get a dozen or so overstock blankets from one department store. Still, it was a start. He decided to check some thrift stores. He found some surprisingly good values, using his birthday money to pick up six kids' coats. Still he wished he could do more.

The good news was Jackson had managed to pool together some cash donations as well as getting promises from some stores for more items. What rankled Taylor was the fact they were the same stores he'd been at. What was it about Jackson Kern that made people fall over themselves to help the guy?

When they put everything together, they had picked up forty-three jackets in assorted sizes, as well as thirty-eight blankets. These were loaded into a volunteer's truck and taken to the shelter. The director cried at the generosity, especially when Jackson handed her a check for $325 he'd collected from businesses and going door-to-door. Everyone agreed: Jackson was just too good to be true. Never before had someone so driven been in charge. He was, without a doubt, king of the school, and Becca always acted as if she were his queen, lording it over the peasants.

An hour before Christmas break was to start, Taylor and five other students were called to the school office. When they arrived they were met by one of the student council representatives, Penny Weiss.

"The student council appreciates the service of everyone. The six of you, however, have exemplified true service and community spirit with your volunteer spirit. With this in mind, we would like to present each of you with a gift. It's just a token of our thanks, really, but we wanted you to know we appreciated your commitment and wanted to thank you for giving back."

Taylor's face warmed. He hadn't expected anything for volunteering. He was surprised anyone even noticed. When Penny handed him the package, Taylor could only mumble his thanks and hope no one would notice his embarrassment. Even though the rest of the students were opening their gifts, Taylor decided he should wait until he got home to open his, though he had to admit he was afraid his curiosity would get the better of him before he even got there. He rushed home, carefully removed the paper, and opened the box. Inside was a hardbound sketchbook. He'd seen them at stores and had really wanted one for himself, but they were pricey, and he couldn't justify spending that much money, no matter how nice the cream-colored paper looked. He ran his hand over the embossed cover, feeling the intricacies of the etching. An envelope fluttered to the floor when he opened the cover of the book. He tore the seal on the envelope and removed the single sheet.

Thank you for your service to the community. It means more than you can know. Jackson Kern.

It wasn't a handwritten note specifically for him, only a photocopy of a general letter, but it made him feel special anyway.

Taylor taped the note to the inside cover of his new sketchbook. He turned to the first clean page and began to draw a picture of the young man who he wanted to imagine was responsible for giving him something so special. By the end of the night he had filled nearly a quarter of the book with pictures of Jackson, playing baseball, sitting in the sun, and laughing. Every nuance lovingly rendered. He fell asleep with the book on the nightstand, open to a picture of Jackson smiling down at him.

TAYLOR went shopping for gifts a few days before Christmas. For his mom he got some lavender-scented oil she really liked, and his dad got a couple of new mysteries he had been asking for. He was trying to figure out what to get for Benny when inspiration struck. He bought backing boards and adhesive, went home and gathered up a few remaining items, and took them to a local photographer. Taylor explained what he wanted to do, and the photographer told him she was impressed. His gift would be truly unique. She set to putting together a display, got Taylor to confirm it met with his approval, and snapped several shots. Taylor was more than happy with the results and hoped the gifts would be well received. He made a couple of phone calls and headed for home.

AT 1:00 P.M. Christmas Eve, the doorbell rang. Taylor, dressed in red-and-green garb with curled shoes adorned with a small silver bell, answered the door to find a shivering Benny standing on the stoop.

"Dude, really? An elf?" Benny asked, quirking an eye.

Taylor glared at his friend. "My folks are having a Christmas party later, and I'm handing out the gifts, okay? Are you going to mock me or come in and get warm?" Taylor asked.

"Warm is good. I like warm," Benny chuckled, taking a deep breath as he stepped into the cinnamon- and pine-scented house.

The house was a winter wonderland, decorated with traditional garlands and lights. The tree stood twinkling, decked out with multicolored tinsel and glittering balls that reflected the light around the room. It was truly breathtaking. Gifts were placed carefully beneath the tree, all wrapped in reflective paper, further adding to the glitz.

"Tay, I love your house, especially during the holidays," Benny said in a hushed voice. "Your folks are always so over-the-top happy. Mine wouldn't know the holiday spirit if Santa himself bit them on their butts."

"I keep forgetting that not everyone has parents like mine. I'm so used to this every year. I can't imagine not having this every year. I'm really glad you're here to share it with me. Mom and Dad are at the neighbors until five o'clock or so. As soon as our other guest comes, I'll give you your presents."

Benny scowled. "Presents? I thought we weren't going to exchange?"

"We're not exchanging. I got you something, though. Why do you think I got dressed already? I wanted to get into character," Taylor explained with a slight smile.

Benny was obviously irritated. "Dude, you can't do that kinda stuff. I wanted to give you something, but you told me no," he snapped.

"I'm still telling you no, but this is something I wanted to do for you guys."

Before Benny could question his meaning, the doorbell sounded again.

"Benny, can you get that?" Taylor asked. He waited, wanting to see his friend's reaction.

Still grumbling, Benny strode to the door and threw it open. He seemed surprised to find Addy Dean there. "Addy?" Benny's jaw dropped for a moment, only to be replaced by a warm smile.

"Hi, Benny. Taylor asked me to come over. Is it okay if I come in?" Addy asked, tugging at the collar of his jacket.

"Yeah, of course," he said, stepping back to allow Addy entry into the house. "Come on in. Let me take your coat."

"Uh... no, thanks. I'm not really staying. He called and asked me to come over, but I'm not sure why he wanted me here."

"Hey, Addy, thanks for stopping over. Why don't you come into the living room with Benny?" Taylor called out.

Addy shuffled over to where Taylor was and just stood, seemingly unsure of what he should do. He smirked when he saw Taylor's outfit but didn't say anything.

"Addy," Taylor said quietly, "I'd really appreciate it if you'd take off your coat and stay for a while."

Addy sighed but removed his jacket, laying it across the chair. Therapy had obviously done him some good. He no longer wore long sleeve shirts buttoned to the neck. Instead he had on a heavy, short-sleeved plaid work shirt, the scars and burns on his arms visible for the world to see.

"Thanks," Taylor started. "I'm glad you both showed up. I've got something for you guys, and I really hope you'll like it."

Addy looked down at his feet.

"I don't have anything for you, I'm sorry. I didn't know—"

"Addy," Taylor interrupted, "this was something I wanted to do. I don't expect anything from you. Okay?"

Addy nodded.

Taylor handed the boxes to Addy and Benny, telling them to open the cards first. They each opened the envelope, and Benny read the identical handwritten message inside aloud: "Our friends each have a piece of us to hold in their hearts."

Taylor saw Addy look to Benny. When their eyes met, Addy gave Benny a small smile, and Benny gave a wide grin in return. They carefully opened the boxes and found inside a jigsaw puzzle and a bottle of puzzle glue. They looked at Taylor curiously.

"I don't understand. What's this supposed to be?" Benny asked, rubbing a hand over his face.

Taylor handed each of them a picture.

"This puzzle is about the friends I have," he began. "Friends that each have a special place in here," he said, pointing to his chest. "I took some of the drawings I did over the summer and put them together with the painting Addy did, then had them photographed and made into a puzzle. Once you've completed it, you can take the puzzle glue and make it a permanent picture. I have backing boards you can put the whole thing together on. I know it sounds kinda lame, but being with you guys for the summer really meant a lot to me, and I hoped you'd enjoy this too."

Benny made his way over to Taylor and pulled him into a hug. Benny and Taylor opened their arms and looked expectantly at Addy. Benny raised his eyebrows, motioned with his head and waited. Addy smiled slightly and stepped into the group hug.

"Thank you, Taylor," Addy said. "This means the world to me."

"Me, too, Tay. I can't begin to tell you how much I love this gift," Benny agreed.

Taylor went to get some cider and cookies for them, pausing for a moment to see his friends chatting by the tree. He smiled. They were a part of his family, and he was happy to have them both there.

JANUARY was blustery and bitter cold in Milwaukee. The temperature barely climbed above three degrees for several weeks in a row. Everyone was grumpy. The inability to go outside for more than a few minutes without getting frostbite was getting under everyone's skin. Jackson announced there was going to be a party in the gym and invited the school to come out to have a good time.

It was incredible. They turned the gymnasium into a beach party. There were burgers and hot dogs, fries, chips, soda pop, balloons, streamers, banners about the upcoming baseball season. It seemed the whole school really had turned out. Taylor was working the concession stand, again. Becca obviously preferred to keep him as far away from the main group of people as possible. He couldn't figure out why she was always the one in charge of the volunteers, but it didn't matter. He was having a good time. Benny had come by and expressed his delight at the fact they even had veggie burgers and were cooking them separately from the meat! It didn't take much to make him happy, apparently.

The music, the dancing, the games, all added up to a great time. People were laughing, playing volleyball, lying out on blankets, and throwing Frisbees. If it wasn't for the basketball nets, the folded bleachers, and the hardwood floors, you could almost think it really was summer and this was a party at Bradford beach.

Jackson and Becca mixed and mingled, being the perfect hosts. Taylor saw Jackson walking toward the concession table, but Jackson seemed to be looking elsewhere.

"Taylor, can I have a white soda?"

"Sure. One sec," Taylor replied, grabbing a plastic cup. As the cup filled, he looked at Jackson, disappointed, but not really surprised, when Jackson wouldn't meet his eyes. "Here you go. Can I get you anything else?"

Jackson gave him a frown and walked away without saying another word. Taylor's heart hurt a little. He knew Jackson hated him, but he thought the guy could at least be tolerant, like he seemed to be with everyone else. They'd never exchanged words, and it saddened Taylor that Jackson could behave this way toward him. He was still crazy about Jackson, but the crushing pain had subsided over the last few months, replaced by a dull ache and calming the overwhelming need he'd always associated with his thoughts of the student council president.

BY THE middle of February, everyone was eagerly talking about the prom. There were tuxes and dresses to be gotten, limos to rent, dinners and motel rooms to make reservations for. All the juniors seemed to be buzzing about it. Benny said he had asked someone but was turned down, so he wouldn't be attending. Taylor asked him who he had wanted as his date, but Benny was noncommittal about it. Still, he pleaded with his friend to come along as a volunteer to keep him company, which Benny grudgingly agreed to do.

The theme this year was going to be "Growing Together," which was, of course, Jackson's idea. The idea of the school, growing together like a community, seemed a perfect fit for what he'd done since he took over as student council president. Taylor realized that, maybe, it was the community Jackson was trying to build that had kept him from being harassed when he was outed. If Jackson and he were talking, maybe he could say "thank you."

CHAPTER NINE
PROM

THE big night finally arrived. Even though it was early spring the air was warm and moist. The stars twinkled and a full moon cast a glow over the school. It was almost magical. The students arrived in their finery, chatted with each other, danced, and generally had a good time.

Taylor was manning the refreshment table… again, but at least Benny was there to keep him company. Benny seemed depressed, but Taylor didn't ask him about it, assuming because he didn't have a date, he wasn't really up for fun. When Jackson and Becca made their entrance, everyone stopped and applauded. She looked beautiful in a royal-blue dress that touched the floor, with a plunging V-cut neckline and some amazing beadwork around the waist. Her hair was done up in a frenzy of curls, and Taylor had to grudgingly admit she looked good. In fact, she was absolutely radiant. Jackson was equally breathtaking. His black suit coat was offset by a dazzlingly blue shirt that was the perfect match to Becca's dress. They looked amazing together, poised and confident, definitely worthy of the prom king and queen titles that were sure to be theirs.

As the night went on, fewer people came to the refreshment table. Benny stepped away to use the restroom, leaving Taylor alone. Not long after, Jackson stepped up.

"Taylor, can I have a white soda, please?"

"Sure thing," Taylor replied, handing the fizzy beverage over.

Jackson turned to leave but stopped after a few steps. Taylor heard him sigh. With his back still toward Taylor, he quietly questioned, "Taylor, what did I do?"

"What do you mean?" Taylor asked, not really following the question.

"I don't really know," Jackson admitted. "I just know I did something to make you hate me. You never talk to me. You always look away. I'm confused as to what I did."

Taylor's jaw dropped, and he gaped at Jackson.

"You did *not* just say that to me. I knew you were many things, Jackson Kern, but I never took you to be a hypocrite," Taylor spit out.

Jackson spun on his heel, his face a jumble of emotions. "What does that mean? Tell me what I did," he insisted. Jackson clenched his hands into tight fists, his anger obvious. "What the hell did I ever do to you?"

"You mean besides calling me disgusting? Besides saying I deserved to get beat up? Besides telling people no one would have me except maybe as a pity fuck? God, I don't know, Jackson. What could you possibly have done?" Taylor shot back.

The color drained from Jackson's face. He was clenching his hands so tightly the knuckles were turning white.

"I… I never said that. Ever. Why would you think that, Taylor?" Jackson asked, head cocked slightly, his frown evident.

"Becca told me what you said!" Taylor railed. "You couldn't stand the sight of me. She told me that—"

"You wanted me to stay as far away from you as possible," Jackson said sadly. "That you couldn't bear looking at me. When she came to you and told you that I…," he faltered, then looked up, his eyes meeting Taylor's, and suddenly he froze for a moment. His mouth tightened and his lips stretched into a sneer, realization setting his face into a twisted mask. "Becca!" he shouted and stormed off.

Scrambling from behind the table, Taylor followed close behind. When they drew near to where Becca was standing, her eyes grew as big as saucers.

"You unbelievable bitch!" Jackson growled, his eyes seething with bitterness.

93

"Jax, what's wrong?" she asked, trying to maintain her poise, eyes darting between Taylor and Jackson.

Between the anger evident on Jackson's face and the frightened look on Becca's, Taylor could see it wasn't going to work for her. Not this time.

"You know damn well what's wrong. I trusted you. My God, I told you things because I thought we were friends."

Becca reached out and grabbed Jackson's arm, but he shrugged her off. "Jackson, you can't want to be with someone like... him," she said, pointing her finger accusingly at Taylor. "You're too good for trash. He won't do anything but bring you down."

Taylor shrank back, struggling to maintain his calm.

"I think I should be the one who decides what I want, Becca, not you. God, I can't believe I was so stupid," Jackson spat, carding his hand through his hair. "You made it so I was *afraid* to talk to him. For almost two years, I thought he hated me because you kept insisting it was true. It used to twist my stomach up in knots every time I saw him, thinking somehow I had done something to make him hate me, and you knew. You fucking knew!" Jackson's voice kept getting louder. Other people were starting to stare. Benny rushed over to where they stood, flanking Taylor.

"You should be with me, Jackson. I'm the one who's always there for you. I'm the one who knows you. You know I care about you," she cooed softly.

"I told you that we could never be more than friends. You aren't the one I want. You were never the one I wanted. You don't care about me. All you ever cared about was your social status. You knew we could never be more than that because I... because I...."

"Don't say it, Jackson," Becca threatened. Then in a softer tone, she said, "We can just forget this happened. Why would you ruin what you have? You're finally accepted. You finally have friends. Isn't that what you always wanted?" she said, as if trying to soothe a child.

"No," Jackson said defiantly. "What I wanted was to belong. I didn't really care how. I don't care about championships or trophies. I care about doing things. I care about helping people. I want to be there for others." He turned and looked longingly at Taylor. "I want someone to see... me," he said sadly.

"Jackson," Benny said, "Taylor does see you. He's always seen you."

Jackson turned his attention to Benny, eyes plainly pleading for him to continue.

Benny stepped closer to Taylor but kept looking directly at Jackson. "For a long time, you're the one thing that has been on his mind. All the volunteering? It was because of you. To help you. To be near you. He wanted so badly to be your friend, but she," he said, giving a curt nod toward Becca, "manipulated him and made him feel like garbage. Even after that? He still did it for you because he wanted you to succeed and was willing to do everything he could to make sure it happened, because he believed in you. Even when he thought you hated him, that you were disgusted by him, he still did all of that for you."

Jackson tilted his head and smiled wryly. "Do you see, Becca? All your hate? It was undone by one act of kindness."

"I know you, Jackson," she growled. "I know your secrets."

"You're right," he admitted. "You do."

Jackson turned and stormed off toward the stage just as the principal approached the microphone.

"We're now going to announce your prom king and queen," he said. "This year we are proud to announce your king will be Jackson Kern and your queen will be Becca Monroe."

A smattering of applause rose from those assembled. Becca began to hurry to the stage, but Jackson made it there first.

"No," he said, grabbing the microphone. "I'm honored, truly, but I will not be accepting this crown."

For a moment it seemed like everyone was stunned into silence. Then the murmuring began, demanding to know what was going on. All eyes were on Jackson.

"Since I was a kid, all I ever wanted was roots, a place to belong. When you made me student council president, I worked hard to make a community where we all would become some kind of family. I never wanted anything more in my life. Tonight I found out someone was working hard to undo every accomplishment we made."

He paused, his eyes surveying the crowd, who were hanging on his every word. "For almost two years, someone made me afraid. Afraid to talk to someone whom I admired. She made me doubt myself, accused someone of hating me, and I allowed her to strip away choices I had, making me believe her lies. You elected this person as queen, and I cannot... will not... stand with her." Jackson cast a withering look at Becca, who shriveled back into the crowd. "Tonight Becca Monroe's lies finally caught up with her, and I found out the person I admire actually does like me, really does want to be my friend. In an effort to keep me under her thumb, she is now threatening to expose my secrets. But I refuse to give her that kind of power over me, so I'm going to share those secrets with you."

The gathered students watched as Jackson took a deep breath, steeling himself for what he was about to say.

"When we came to Milwaukee, my dad promised me this was going to be our last move until I graduated, and I was thrilled. Because we were never in one place for any length of time, I never felt like I belonged or would be accepted, not really. It's all I ever wanted. I joined the baseball team so I could be a part of something." The pain in his expression made Taylor's heart ache.

He paused once more, his eyes scanning the crowd. Another breath and he plowed on.

"I told Becca tonight what I really wanted was to have someone notice *me*. That's true, it is what I really wanted, but I wanted them to see me the way I often wished Taylor would. And those are the secrets she threatened me with. She assumed I was ashamed of being gay. That was never the case; it just never seemed important. I thought she was my friend, and I was happy to have that, but now I know it wasn't true. She just wanted to use me."

Taylor gasped. The tears that had been threatening now burst forth. His head was spinning. Jackson was gay? Jackson liked him? Really liked him?

"So while you've honored me by voting me as the homecoming king, I won't share the dance with the queen. If you don't mind, I'd really like to share it with a friend."

Jackson slowly stepped toward Taylor, extending his hand. Taylor blushed and held out his own. Jackson pulled him in and together they began to move. The students around them stood stock still, trying to make sense of everything they'd just heard. Some of them drew away, not wanting to bear witness to what was going on. Others shrugged and moved onto the dance floor, joining the king and his consort in the dance.

Jackson whispered to Taylor, "That's not all the secrets. There's some I didn't share with Becca, but I'd like to share them with you. Can we talk later? Please?"

Taylor closed his eyes, put his head on Jackson's shoulder, and nodded, content in the moment.

WILL PARKINSON

CHAPTER TEN
TRUTH AND LIES

SOMETIME during Jackson's speech Becca disappeared, seemingly too humiliated by Jackson exposing her to stay at the dance. Taylor feared there would be hell to pay for it down the road, but right now he couldn't find it in himself to care.

After everyone else had left the dance, Benny came to Taylor, hugged him hard, and told him, "Now if you mess this up, you only have yourself to blame."

Taylor's hands were clammy and he felt queasy, and Benny was making it worse. "Thanks, Benny, that goes a long way to soothing my nerves."

"Half the battle is done already. He likes you. Now you just need to make him love you. It won't be hard, believe me," Benny whispered in a soothing voice. He gave Taylor a little push in Jackson's direction.

Taylor pulled his jacket tight around him and slowly made his way to where Jackson was waiting. A light snow fell, blanketing everything. Against the streetlights it looked like a snow globe. To Taylor it seemed like he was in a dream. He was almost afraid to talk to Jackson, scared he'd wake up to find it had all been nothing more than a dream. It would crush him.

Jackson opened the door of his truck, helped Taylor into the passenger seat, and went to the driver's side and slid into his seat. He didn't look at Taylor, just stared straight ahead. He drew a deep breath before launching into the conversation.

"I need you to understand why I'm telling you this, Taylor. I have never shared this much of myself with anyone. I never wanted

99

to. Over the last two years, I got it into my head we could be together, even though I thought you hated me," Jackson admitted. "I feel stupid now that I know the truth, because it's something that should have been obvious all along. Actually, it *was* obvious, but I was too afraid to take a chance. I never let anyone into my life like this, not even Becca. I thought she was a friend, but she could never be the one I shared everything with. Does that make sense to you?"

Taylor nodded. It made perfect sense. He thought back to the times he'd seen Jackson and Becca together, realizing Jackson never touched her or kissed her in any way that could ever be mistaken for love. He was ashamed he'd let Becca get into his head like that.

"My mom left when I was four," Jackson said. "She decided she didn't want to be stuck with me and my dad because we never stayed anywhere long enough for her to feel at home. I think that's where I get it from. All my life growing up, I'd be in a school for, maybe, six months or so. The longest was a year, back when I was ten or eleven. I never bothered to try and get to know people after second grade, because I knew we weren't going to be there very long. I stopped making close friends because it hurt too much to leave them behind," he said with a wistful sigh. "It was better if I just stayed to myself. Growing up and being the new kid in every school sucked. You were constantly teased, never belonged to a group, couldn't really fit in anywhere."

Taylor listened, being careful not to interrupt. He could tell by Jackson's expression this was something he needed to say and really wanted to get off his chest.

"When I was in sixth grade, we were in Los Angeles. That was the worst year for me, ever. I realized I was gay, and that made me feel doubly alone, because I had no friends to talk with, no mom at home, and there was no way I could talk to my dad. I started going online and reading and joining chat boards for gay kids. That made me feel a little better, but still I never made real friends, flesh-and-blood people who could hug me when I was feeling bad, someone who would love me. I became depressed. My dad wanted me to talk to someone, but with us moving around all the time, we just never got around to it."

Jackson stopped for a moment, his eyes locked on to the steering wheel, hands running over the rough surface of the covering.

"When I was twelve, my mom died. She'd gone out and gotten so drunk one night that when they found her car...." Jackson shuddered at the memory. "Well, it wasn't easy to get her separated from the vehicle. She was already gone, died instantly when she ran into a bridge abutment. The police estimated she was doing sixty in a thirty-mile-an-hour zone, fell asleep, and...."

His breathing hitched a few times before he continued. "That was the lowest point in my life. I was just becoming a teenager, realized I was gay, had no friends, a father who was never there, and now no mom. And it was weird, you know? I mean, I hadn't seen her since she left, but I always held out hope one day she'd come get me and take me to live with her. I'd be able to have a normal life, but that dream went up in smoke."

He fell silent for a moment. Taylor watched him trying to breathe evenly, and he held his own breath, feeling sure something was coming, something important.

"It got so bad that I considered suicide. A couple times." Jackson's eyes met Taylor's. "I never did anything," he added quickly, "but I felt like I could, you know? There were times my dad would go out of town on a business trip, and I'd be home alone for a few days and just thought how easy it would be to just give up. The next day I'd wake up, and the whole cycle would start again."

Jackson's voice dropped, and he turned away from Taylor. "It took me over a year to come to terms with being gay, but I stayed so hidden in the closet that I got further away from people. Then I wasn't just the new kid, I was the freak and weirdo. That amped up the teasing. It was so easy to pick on the fag emo kid because he never fought back. Of course, no one knew I was gay, but anyone different is an automatic fag." He sighed.

Jackson's gaze returned to Taylor, his eyes moist. The glow from the streetlights let Taylor see the hope in Jackson's eyes, pleading for him to understand, to not reject him outright. Taylor placed his hand on Jackson's arm and smiled at him, giving him permission to continue.

"After that it was off to another school. I don't even remember where this one was. Some small hick town my dad got stuck in upgrading a computer system. It was terrible there. The kids were nasty and vindictive, hated anything different from them. That's where I started working out, building myself up because I was tired of being the victim. I tried to change my attitude… at least, the one they saw. Inside I was still terrified, but I tried to keep it under wraps. I figured I could tuck it away in my closet to keep the rest of me company."

The truck was chilly, and Taylor could feel the cold seeping into his legs. He didn't want to say anything. He didn't want Jackson to stop talking, but he couldn't stop the shiver that went through him. Jackson saw it and that brought him up short.

"I'm so sorry, Taylor. I'm an idiot. I should just take you home."

"No, please," Taylor whispered, putting his hand on Jackson's arm. "I don't want to go. I want to talk with you some more. Can we just go somewhere? Maybe get something to eat or drink? Really, Jackson, I need to hear this. If it's easier for you, we can stay in the truck. I don't mind. Maybe we could just turn the heat back on?" he asked hopefully.

Jackson chuckled. His grin was lopsided and so adorable.

"Something to eat would be good. Denny's is open all night. Would that be okay with you?"

"Anywhere is fine, really."

They drove together in companionable silence. On opening the restaurant door, they were greeted with a blast of warm air that carried the scents of bacon and hash browns. Taylor's stomach growled.

"Evening, guys. Two of you tonight?" the waitress asked.

"Yes, ma'am," Jackson replied. "Would it be okay if we sat in the booth in the back corner?"

Fortunately the restaurant was slow. The waitress smiled, directed them to the secluded spot, and handed them their menus. "My name's Elaine, and I'll be taking care of you guys tonight. I'll let you take a look at the menu for a few minutes, and then I'll get your order."

Jackson let Taylor slide into the booth before he slid in next to him.

"I'd like to hear the rest of your story, if you're ready," Taylor told Jackson.

Jackson took a deep breath and let it out slowly. "I told you that I was going to change my attitude. Part of that was I started working out. As I bulked up, kids became afraid of me," Jackson continued. "Most of them stopped harassing me and left me alone, which was great, but I was still really lonely. There was never anyone I really wanted to be with. It was always be picked on or be left alone."

Elaine stopped at the table and gazed at them. "You two are so cute together," she said. "Did you have prom tonight?"

Taylor flushed.

"We did, but we weren't together," Jackson said.

"Oh, I'm sorry. I didn't mean to imply anything by it."

"It's not a problem at all. Really. I'm glad you think we make a good couple because that's what I'm hoping for," Jackson said proudly.

Taylor's face heated even further. Even the tips of his ears were warm. It all seemed to be happening so fast. Everything he'd hoped for, thought he could never have, was right there in front of him, and he was completely overwhelmed.

Elaine smiled wide at Taylor's reaction. She reached over and patted him on the shoulder, giving him a warm smile, like she was letting him know everything was okay. She took their orders and hustled off to the kitchen.

"I'm sorry, I didn't mean to embarrass you." Jackson smiled.

"No, you didn't. I'm just a little overwhelmed. You have to admit this was all pretty surprising. It was a good surprise, though. Go ahead with your story."

"Right. So, I was only at that school for three months, and it was the first one I was really glad to get out of," Jackson stated somewhat harshly.

Taylor assumed something bad had happened, but wasn't sure he should press the issue. He waited for Jackson to continue.

"About a month before I left there, this guy, Alex, kept bugging me. He was seventeen, I was only fourteen. He kept telling me he loved me. He'd touch me when we were alone. Nothing sexual, just putting his hand on my back or arm. It was... nice. I started to appreciate it. I really started to feel he cared about me." Jackson laughed bitterly. "He didn't."

Taylor could see the tears welling up in Jackson's eyes. He moved closer in the booth and put his hand on his friend's knee. Jackson looked over and gave Taylor a weak smile.

"It was all about him making me admit I was gay. Once he did he spread it all over the school. The area we were in? Yeah, it didn't go over so well. I thought I had seen the worst in people, but I was totally unprepared for this. They threw things at me, they spit on me, and they defaced my locker. One guy, while we were in the gym showers, tried to piss on me." Jackson grimaced. "But I never lashed out. Not once. I had never been in a fight, and I really didn't ever want to be. I was just grateful when my dad's assignment ended, and we moved again."

Elaine brought their food, ending their conversation, and they ate silently. Taylor figured Jackson was grateful for the break. His story was hard enough to hear, but to have to tell it? Taylor didn't think he'd be able to make it through anything like that. What he'd had to go through would have been unbearable without Benny in his life. Jackson had no one.

Taylor fumbled with his napkin for a minute. "I have to tell you, Jackson, everything you went through? I don't think I could have done it. You've gotten so confident, and I really admire that."

"When I was fifteen, we went to Chicago. That was the game changer for me. I was the new kid, but it was a big school, and there were a lot of other new kids too. In gym I found I was good at baseball. I also found out there were other gay kids there. I got to be… not friends, really, more like acquaintances, but I could talk with them, learn from them."

Jackson's eyes met Taylor's, and he smiled.

"It was like the whole world opened up for me. In the nine months I was there, my whole attitude changed. I found I really wanted to be a part of something, you know? Something big. Something lasting. I wanted to be there for other people, like I wanted someone to be there for me. I learned everything I could about what I wanted to do with my life, who I wanted to be," he said, smiling proudly.

It only lasted a few moments before the smile faded.

"When Dad told me we were moving again, I was devastated. I thought I'd finally gotten a handle on things, but then we came here. This time, though, Dad told me we would be staying. He'd gotten a job helping a firm downtown revamp their entire computer network, and it would take a couple of years to complete the whole thing. That meant we'd be staying until I graduated. I was overwhelmed. I realized I could finally be a part of something, make something of myself, and find a way to help other people."

Jackson shook his head.

"The first time I walked into Mrs. Wagner's homeroom, I had to stop outside the door and tell myself it should be easier now, as many times as I'd done it, but it really wasn't. When Mrs. Wagner connected me with Becca, I felt like it was a whole new beginning. Then I joined the baseball team, and that's where I got to see you. I couldn't figure out what you were doing there. You seemed so out of place. Then I'd see you at every practice and every game, always standing in the same spot, watching and cheering for us. It got to the point where I expected, I needed to see you there, and things just didn't seem to go right if you weren't."

"I used to go there to watch you. When you first walked into class, the first thought I had was that I needed to sketch you, so I wouldn't forget the look on your face. You were nervous, but you just seemed so determined. I admired that and was drawn to it. I wanted to be there for you."

Jackson picked up a french fry and swirled it in ketchup for a moment before he looked back up at Taylor.

"When we had the tournament in Beloit, I was all kinds of messed up because there seemed to be something missing. When you showed up, I felt calm and relieved, like a great weight had been lifted from my shoulders. Everything clicked into place again. I used to step out onto the field and look at the crowd just so I could see you. I used to wave at everyone, but it was meant for you, to let you know that I saw you and that it calmed me. I really wanted to talk with you and ask why you kept showing up if you... well, if you hated me, but I was terrified that if I said anything you'd just"— Jackson made a gesture with his hands—"disappear, poof, and nothing would ever be right again."

Taylor wiped his sleeve across his eye and smiled at Jackson. "I think that's the sweetest thing I've ever heard," he said quietly.

"It's true. In fact, when things were going well for the team and all the stuff with the council, I started realizing that maybe I *could* finally have someone in my life and I wouldn't lose them too. When I found out that you cared for me, I found myself wishing it would be you. At least, I hope I won't lose you." Jackson looked at Taylor, longing and sadness in his eyes.

"Thank you for trusting me, Jackson. I want you to know... this means so much to me, being here with you. It's something I've dreamed about. And you need to know I will always be here for you. I'll never let you be alone again."

Taylor put his right hand on Jackson's sleeve and peered into his eyes.

Jackson reached out and put his hand on Taylor's neck, drawing him in for a kiss. It was completely different than when

Kevin had kissed him. It was sweet, warm, and done with emotion, not just a driving need to take possession.

"I was right," Elaine sighed. "You do make the most adorable couple."

Jackson looked up and laughed with Elaine.

"Can I get you guys any dessert?" she asked.

"None for me, thanks," Taylor said.

"I'm almost all done in too," Jackson answered. "I'm just gonna pick at this for a bit."

She laid the check on the table, wished them a good night, and left. Jackson looked down, his fingers fidgeting against the table, his lip curled downward.

"There's one more thing, Taylor," he said quietly. "This isn't something I'm proud of, and I hope it's something you can forgive."

Taylor watched him quietly. He could see Jackson was struggling with what he wanted to say.

"Whatever it is, Jackson, I'm sure it's going to be okay."

Jackson took a deep breath, appearing to center himself before he spoke again.

"After what happened to you… well, Kevin told Cody you had been responsible for it. Mitch told some of the guys on the team, me included. I didn't believe it was true. I never did. I went to see you while you were in the hospital. You were really out of it. I sat by your bed and held your hand. I made a promise to you I would take care of it. Then I hugged you and left. I'm not sure why I did it. Since I figured you hated me, it would have been easier to just let it go, but I didn't hate you, and I really wanted to protect you. I asked Mitch about Kevin and went to see him."

Taylor began breathing heavily. He knew where this was going, and he didn't like it, not at all.

"When I got to Kevin's house, he invited me in. We talked for a bit, and then he asked me to come up to his room. When we got there, he got grabby. When I told him I wasn't interested, he said, 'You're a fucking tease, just as bad as Taylor.' I snapped, and I demanded to know why he lied about what had happened. He laughed and said you were a slut, and you had wanted it, but then you became a cockteaser, and that pissed him off. I told him he was going to tell the truth about what happened and make it right. He swung at me, and I… I swung back," Jackson confessed.

Taylor could see the pain on Jackson's face. His eyes were shiny, and he swallowed hard before he continued.

"I'd never been in a fight, Taylor. This wasn't really a fight anyway. He went down with one hit, but I didn't stop. I hit him in the face over and over again, until he begged me to stop. My hands were bruised. When I realized what I did, oh God, I was so ashamed. But he had hurt you, and I needed to hurt him back." Jackson looked down at his hands, fingers twisting nervously. "I broke his nose, Taylor. I broke it and I didn't care. I grabbed him by the shirt collar and told him he would fix it, or I'd report him for sexual assault. I left him lying on the floor, blood pouring out of his nose. I'm so sorry."

Taylor's face grew warm. His eyes widened. "You did that for me?"

"Yeah," Jackson replied sheepishly. "And I'd do it again, because you meant more to me than even I realized until that moment. I was grateful you weren't in school for the week, because my hands were bruised and hurting. Becca wanted to know what happened. I just told her I'd had an accident and everything was okay. I know it didn't fix anything, and you were still outed, but it was all I could do—"

Taylor gave a small smile. "Actually, I think you helped a lot. What you accomplished with the student council? I think it helped with the attitudes at school. I thought it was going to be a lot worse than it was, and I'm pretty sure that was due to you."

Jackson's face broke into the cutest goofy grin. Taylor, however, couldn't return the happy look.

"Jackson, while I'm touched that you did that for me… you could have made it worse. They could have filed charges against you. You could have gotten arrested."

Jackson looked chastised. "I know. I lost my cool, and that never happened before. I wish to hell it hadn't happened now, but I can't undo it. I'll understand if you want not to see me. I don't want that, but I could understand it."

"No, Jackson. Never that. I don't like that you did it, but I know you did it for me. That makes me feel… safe. The only other person in my life who makes me feel like that is Benny."

"So now you know my history. What about yours? What is there to know about Taylor Andrews?"

Taylor took a deep breath. "Where to begin? I've lived in Milwaukee my whole life. My mom works as a front desk clerk at the Pfister, a hotel downtown. My dad's a web designer. You already know Benny is my best friend."

While he spoke Taylor doodled nervously on the back of the placemat, doing a picture of his friends and family. He noticed Jackson watching his hands as they worked.

"You're amazingly good," Jackson said quietly. "I like seeing your face when you draw. I can see you focusing on what you're doing, even if your mind is somewhere else." He paused. "So continue your story."

Taylor smiled. He liked the fact Jackson appreciated his work. "Benny was the first person I came out to. It was the hardest thing I've ever done in my life. I'd known for a while, but every time I saw him, all kinds of things went through my head. I was worried he'd take it badly, maybe be angry with me. Most of all I was really afraid I'd lose him as my best friend. We were in my bedroom one day, and I kept trying to figure out a way to bring it up. Benny wasn't even looking at me. I can't remember what he was doing. I think he was reading, but he asked me, 'What's going on in your head? You've got your thinking face on.' It was the first time he'd ever mentioned it. I couldn't figure out what to say to him. I was embarrassed."

Taylor paused for a moment, took a sip of water, and then continued.

"It took a few minutes before I finally just blurted it out and told him I was gay. He looked at me like I'd grown another head or something."

Jackson laughed. "What did he say?"

"He looked at me very seriously for a minute before shrugging his shoulders and saying, 'Yeah? So?'"

"That's it?" Jackson snickered. "All that buildup and that's all you got? That was kind of disappointing."

"I know. By the time I finished telling him, I had tears in my eyes, I was so nervous, and he just made it all better with those two simple words."

"I can see why you like him. He seems like a really cool guy."

"He is, but don't tell him that. He already has a swelled head," Taylor said jokingly.

"Do you think maybe you could introduce us one day? I'd really like to meet him."

"I'd be happy to. I know he'd like that," Taylor said.

"I'd really like for he and I to be friends. I want to be with you, Taylor. I want to know everything I can about you. I want to learn what makes you smile and be there to see it happen," Jackson stated matter-of-factly.

"I'd like that too. Thank you for letting me in, Jackson. I don't think I've ever felt more comfortable with anyone other than Benny before."

"Taylor, I really do care about you. I have for the longest time. Seeing you became the focal point of my day. As long as I knew you were there, everything was going to be okay. It would always frustrate me when I tried to talk to you, and you would turn away. I understand why now, but when it happened, it really hurt a lot," Jackson told him, the anguish registering in his voice.

Taylor gave a sympathetic smile. "Yeah, Becca really did a number on both of us, didn't she?"

Nodding, Jackson ate the last bite of his sandwich. "I'm really sorry about her, Taylor. I wish I hadn't trusted her. I told her how I felt about you, and she played me big time. She told me she'd feel you out, see if you felt the same way. She told me you didn't, and then gave me nothing but lies."

He paused briefly. Taylor knew the question he wanted to ask above all others. He knew if he didn't ask now he might never do it.

"Jackson, I have to know… why were you at my house? I got a version from Becca when she told me that you came to my house to tell me you were disgusted by me and didn't want anything to do with me, which killed me by the way, but I'm sure it was just another one of her lies."

Jackson grinned. "I came over to talk to you. I saw you at the tournament. We were losing, and after you got there, I was able to focus again. I… I came to your house to say thanks. To tell you what you did for me. I mean, she told me you didn't want me, but I still felt like I needed to talk to you myself. I wish I had. We could have saved ourselves a lot of problems."

"Well, maybe next time we'll know better, huh?" Taylor asked pensively.

"Next time? I have you now, Taylor Andrews, and I'll be damned if I'm going to give you up for anything," Jackson declared, a sly smile on his face.

"Mr. Kern, I'm going to hold you to that," Taylor replied with an equally cheeky grin. "Let's get out of here."

They paid the bill, Jackson leaving Elaine a very hefty tip, and got back into the truck. Taking Taylor's hand in his, Jackson pulled it to his chest.

"Thank you, Taylor. Thanks for talking with me. I feel a lot better knowing you're there with me. It's the first time in my life I have a special someone to share things with, and it's really great."

"I'm really glad too," Taylor said with a smile. But even knowing they were finally together, he was nervous. They would still have to contend with Becca, and who knew what she'd do?

CHAPTER ELEVEN

SUFFERING

MONDAY morning, Taylor opened the door to Jackson's truck. His stomach fluttered just a little when Jackson smiled at him. After buckling in, Taylor slumped in the seat.

"Are you ready for this?" Jackson asked.

"Do I have a choice?" was Taylor's mumbled reply.

"You always have a choice. We can go in together, not letting them get to us, or we can go in separately and let other people win. It's up to you how you want to handle it." Jackson reached over and took Taylor's hand. "I know which one I'm going for."

Taylor took a deep breath, exhaled slowly, and announced, "Yeah, let's do it."

They drove the rest of the way in silence. Taylor's mind was all over the place. While he wanted to be calm for Jackson, inside, his stomach was clenching, and he clamped his jaws tight to keep his teeth from chattering. He kept stealing glances at Jackson, annoyed at his calm attitude.

"It's okay, I'm nervous too," Jackson admitted.

At the door to the school, Jackson held out a hand and looked at Taylor. Taking another deep breath, Taylor took Jackson's hand, and they walked in as a couple. Taylor noticed people staring at them, some of them making faces as if they were going to be sick, others smiling or giving them small, encouraging signs.

Becca pointedly ignored Jackson and Taylor. When she saw them enter the school, she turned and stomped off in the opposite direction. After homeroom, Jackson gave Taylor a quick kiss and moved on to his next class. Taylor's knees were wobbly, especially when Jackson glanced back and shot him a lopsided grin. He wanted to pinch himself, just to see if it was real. The hard smack to the back of his head answered that question, though.

"Don't you fags know you shouldn't do that kind of stuff around normal people?" Larry Dykstra snapped.

Taylor shivered. He should have known they'd wait till he was alone. He should never have done this. His heart raced, and his mouth felt dry. He would try to ignore Larry, but he was sure it would just draw more attention.

"What's the matter, Larry? Jealous? You need a hug or something?" a voice boomed from behind. Taylor grinned and turned to Larry.

"Hi, Benny. What's going on?" Taylor asked, his pulse steadying.

"Came to walk you to class. Figured since I was heading that way we could talk."

"Aw, isn't that sweet? You two would be so cute together," Larry mocked.

Benny stepped in closer to Larry, looking down at him.

"Only gonna say this once, Larry, so make sure you listen to me very carefully," Benny snarled. "I don't like bullies. I can't stand people who pick on anyone, but if you mess with my friends again, you and I *will* have problems. If I hear from anybody that you've been giving them crap, we may have to have this conversation outside of school. You *do* understand what I mean, right, Larry?"

Taylor saw Larry flinch and hold up his hands.

"Sure, I understand. I didn't mean anything by it," he groveled. Turning to Taylor he extended a hand. "I'm really sorry. I won't... you know... bug you or anything again," he stuttered.

Taylor looked at Larry's hand. He was going to refuse to shake, but Benny pinned him with a stare.

"Taylor? Larry's trying to apologize. I think the least you can do is accept, don't you?" Benny said calmly.

Grudgingly Taylor took Larry's hand, noticing how clammy it was. He suppressed a grin of satisfaction at how uncomfortable Larry looked.

"We're good," Taylor said with a slight smile.

Larry hustled down the hall. Benny put a meaty hand on Taylor's shoulder.

"I'm thinking he's not going to cause you any more problems." Benny snickered.

"I thought for sure he was gonna wet himself."

"Yeah, I was kind of hoping for it too," Benny admitted. "You want me to walk with you to class?"

Taylor smiled at his friend. "Thanks, Benny. I think I can do this. It's easier knowing you've got my back."

"Told you I would." He laughed, ruffling Taylor's curls.

Taylor only saw Jackson a few times that day, but each time Jackson would acknowledge him with a wink or a wave. If they were in close enough proximity, he'd give him a hug, Taylor enjoying the brief closeness.

Over the next several weeks, they fell into a routine. Jackson would drive Taylor to school, and they would chat about student council, plans for their senior year, the way they'd been treated by some of their classmates who were, by and large, very accepting, which Taylor believed was due to either Jackson's popularity or Benny's presence.

One day after class, Taylor invited Jackson back to his house to meet his parents. He had explained to them the morning after the dance what had happened, and they were dying to meet the young man who had so easily stolen their son's heart. Jackson was leery but agreed to come over. When they arrived, Taylor's mom greeted Jackson with a warm smile, and his father offered a firm handshake.

"So, Jackson," Taylor's mom began, "what are your intentions toward my son?"

Taylor groaned. "*Mooooooom*," he whined.

His parents cracked up.

"Mrs. Andrews, my intentions are to have Taylor in my life. I want his day to start with a smile and his night to end with a full heart," Jackson said with all sincerity.

Taylor thought the startled expression on his mother's face was priceless. He knew she was joking when she asked the question, but he could tell the answer meant a lot to her when she swept Jackson up in a crushing hug.

"Be careful around this one. He's quite the charmer," she said as she released Jackson, but the wide smile on her face remained.

"He's definitely that," Taylor agreed, giving Jackson a wink.

Taylor showed Jackson his room, smiling when Jackson stopped just inside, letting his eyes wander. That smile turned to embarrassment when Jackson grinned and pointed to something across the room.

"It's a cool room, but I think you might have missed a little something over there."

Taylor's gaze moved to where Jackson was pointing, a burst of heat flaring through his face as he noticed a pair of underwear that had missed the hamper laying bunched up in the corner.

"Oh God," Taylor moaned. He pushed his way past Jackson and hurried to move the garment into the laundry basket. He did a quick check, rushing around trying to straighten up anything that might cause him further mortification. When he was finally satisfied the room wasn't a disaster area, he turned his attention back to Jackson, who was leafing through the sketchbook that was filled with images of him.

"Wow," Jackson said, awe evident in his voice. "These are amazing. When I saw it, I knew I had to get it for you. It seemed like the perfect gift."

"This came from you?"

Jackson nodded. "I wanted you to have it, but I thought you hated me. I knew I couldn't just give it to you, so I had Penny give it to you along with the other gifts from the council. I *needed* you to have this book. Just looking at it shows me how much it means to you, and I'm so glad. These pictures? Knowing that you were thinking of me makes me feel special, and it makes this gift so much more precious because of it. Thank you, Taylor."

"I love that book. It was one of the nicest gifts I've ever gotten. Thank you so much for knowing what it would mean to me," Taylor replied.

Jackson put the book back on the nightstand and pulled Taylor to him. He ran his fingers through Taylor's curly hair, moving their lips together into a soft, gentle kiss. Taylor's eyes closed, and he put his arms around Jackson's waist.

"Taylor?" his mom called out. "Would you and Jackson like to have a snack?"

Taylor stepped back and grinned at Jackson. "Can we pick this up later?"

Jackson gave him a wide smile and a nod, then took his hand and went back downstairs to visit with Taylor's parents.

As he and Jackson sat talking to his parents, Taylor's phone rang. He glanced down, and his heart began to pound erratically, causing his chest to ache when he read the name displayed on the screen. "I'll be right back," he said, quickly moving into the other room.

He flipped open the phone and answered very brusquely.

"What do you want, Kevin?"

"Hi to you, too, Taylor. Miss me?"

"You're kidding, right? What do you want?"

"Pretty sure you know what I want, Taylor. I know about you and your new lover boy. You know that's not going to work, right? You're mine, Taylor. Always will be."

Taylor snorted. "You're deluded. You mean nothing to me, you never did, you never will."

"Aw, babe, don't be like that. We had a small disagreement. That's all it was. You know I never meant to hurt you."

"I'm going to hang up now, Kevin. Don't call here again."

"You probably don't want to do that, Taylor. Actually, you *really* don't want to do that," Kevin snarled.

Taylor's heartbeat went into triple time. "What do you want, Kevin?"

"You're going to come back to me, Taylor. You belong to me. You're going to come back, and it's going to be perfect, just like it should have always been. It's gonna be *sooooo* good."

Taylor felt his nausea rising. "And why do you think I'd do something so stupid?"

"If you want your *boyfriend*"—he spat the word—"to stay safe, yeah, I think you will. And if I were you, I wouldn't tell anyone about this, either."

Taylor froze. "What do you mean?"

"Tell you what, babe, you meet me tomorrow, and we'll talk about it. I've got something you should see. How's that sound?"

"I'm not meeting you, Kevin. There's no way in hell."

"Taylor, sweetheart, you're going to want to see what I have," came the icy reply. "Let's just say that you and Jackson both have a lot riding on it."

Taylor swallowed hard. The tone of Kevin's voice told Taylor to take him seriously. After what Kevin had done to him, he was afraid of what else he might be capable of.

"Fine, we'll talk, but I'm not going anywhere with you. I'll meet you at Sheridan Park after school. I'll be by the pavilion."

"That works for me, Taylor. See you tomorrow. Sweet dreams."

Taylor slipped his phone into his pants pocket and returned to his parents and Jackson. The smile on Jackson's face faded quickly when he saw Taylor. He rushed over to him, putting an arm around his waist to steady him.

"What's wrong? You're shaking," Jackson said, his voice soft. Taylor's parents joined them, his mother clutching his face in her hands.

She gasped. "You're so pale."

"I'm… just not feeling really good. I think I'm going to go lay down. I'm sorry, Jackson. Maybe we can do this another time?"

"Yeah, of course. Are you going to be okay? Do you need something?"

"No, I'm fine. I think I just need to sleep for a while."

Jackson gave him a quick squeeze and said his good-byes before leaving the house. Taylor's mom marched him upstairs, telling him she'd check on him later. After she closed the door, Taylor drew the pillow to his face and cried.

ALTHOUGH he'd gone to bed early, he hadn't slept very well. The conversation with Kevin played over and over in his head as Taylor tried to figure out what he was going to do. When he arrived at the pavilion, he spotted Kevin. He blew out several deep breaths, trying to steady his nerves. He was thankful there were plenty of other people around, since he doubted Kevin would do anything in public. He made his way toward the pavilion, making sure to stay in sight of others. When he got to where Kevin stood, he got a dark glare that chilled him.

"Glad you could make it, Taylor. Let's sit down," he said, leering.

Kevin led Taylor to one of the picnic tables and sat across from him. He pulled out a manila envelope and slid it across the table. Taylor picked it up and hesitated.

Kevin stuffed his hands into his pockets and glared at Taylor. "Open it, babe. It should explain everything to you."

Trembling fingers unsealed the envelope. The contents spilled out onto the table. There were several pictures of Jackson, taken at different places, all of them showing him relaxed, unconcerned.

"Where did you get these?" Taylor demanded.

"Let's just say after our… visit, I've been keeping tabs on Jackson. Have been for a while now. Those are just a few of the pictures I have." Kevin smirked. "Here's how it's going to work, Taylor. I'm sure you know what he did to me. You were mine first. You should have been with me." Kevin's voice remained scary calm. "Then he came along and whipped my ass, telling me you were going to be his." Kevin's voice broke. "So I'm gonna take away something important from him. You have a choice. Either you break up with him and come back to where you belong, or else Jackson may have… serious problems he might not see coming. And you try to tell anyone? Yeah, that's gonna cause him problems too."

"You leave him alone!" Taylor snapped.

"Look, Taylor, you're gonna be with me. That's just how it is. If it wasn't for Jackson, you'd have been mine. You know it's true. And I still want you. I've always wanted you." Kevin's eyes darkened. "If it hurts Jackson at the same time? Well, that's just a bonus."

Taylor looked at Kevin, defiance burning in his eyes.

"You can't do this, Kevin."

"S'up to you, babe. You know what you need to do." Taylor saw Kevin stiffen. "Call me. Love you," he warbled.

Kevin quickly gathered up the pictures and hurried away. Taylor's mind was racing. *Call the police,* his mind screamed. He realized that wouldn't keep Jackson safe. After what Jackson had done to Kevin, it might get him in trouble too. He didn't know what to do. He had to grab the picnic table to steady himself when his knees buckled. His heart hammered, feeling like it might burst from his chest. He wanted to run, flee everything to protect the people he loved. He flinched when he felt a strong hand grip his shoulder and spun quickly to find Jackson staring at him.

"Taylor? Are you all right? You look awful."

"What—what are you doing here?" Taylor managed to stammer.

"I usually come down here to run by the lake. Are you okay?"

"Uh… yeah, I'm okay. I just have a really bad headache. I think I'm going to go home and lay down for a while, okay?"

"I can give you a ride if you want," Jackson said, a worried look etched on his face.

"No, I'm good, thanks."

Jackson bent to give him a kiss, but Taylor stepped out of range.

"If I'm coming down with something, I don't want you to get it. I'll see you tomorrow, all right?" he said quickly.

Jackson looked at him curiously but said, "Sure, I hope you feel better."

When he returned home, Taylor fled to his room. He wanted desperately to call Benny, but Kevin's threat brought him up short. Taylor felt trapped. He didn't want to give up Jackson after they finally found each other, but he couldn't take the chance Kevin would hurt him, either. Everything was so messed up. He fell onto the bed, clutching the pillow to his chest, and sobbed, knowing he had no real choice at all.

TAYLOR tried to look anywhere but at Jackson. He could see the other students pulling into the school's parking lot, and he wished what he was about to do was just part of a bad dream.

"Jackson," Taylor said softly, not daring to look into the deep brown eyes, "I don't think I can do this. I don't think I can see you anymore."

"Taylor? Why? What did I do?"

Taylor's heart broke as he saw Jackson's chest heaving, tears forming in his eyes and spilling over onto his cheeks.

"Nothing. I just… I don't really think I want a relationship. I don't think I'm ready for it," Taylor told him, looking out the window so he wouldn't see Jackson's face.

"We can go slow, Taylor. We don't have to rush into anything," Jackson pleaded.

Taylor glanced over and saw Jackson's jaw quivering. Taylor knew Jackson was on the verge of breaking down, and he couldn't watch it happen. He couldn't see the man he cared so deeply for, and had just hurt so badly, fall apart.

Taylor touched the handle of the truck, looked down, and quietly said, "No, it's better if we just let it go, Jackson. I'm sorry."

"You swore you weren't going to leave me, Taylor. Please. Don't leave," Jackson begged in ragged breaths.

Taylor couldn't contain his sobs. He threw open the door and fled toward the school. The truck engine roared to life and tires squealed as Jackson sped away. Taylor turned back, but Jackson was already out of the lot and gone.

"Oh God, what have I done?" He broke down.

BY THE end of the day, Jackson still hadn't returned to school. Taylor fretted about where Jackson was, but he knew in his heart he was doing the only thing he could to keep his man safe. He kept seeing the shattered look on Jackson's face and knew the betrayal he must have felt. Taylor felt like his heart had been ripped from his chest, and it was worse because he, himself, had been the one who tore it out.

When he got home, he went to his room and took out his cell. He steeled himself for the conversation that was about to happen.

"Well, hello, love," Kevin chirped.

"You don't get to call me that!"

"Baby, I will call you whatever I want. I told you, you're mine. Or am I going to have to... visit with our good friend Jackson?"

"No," Taylor said, fearful of the implied threat. Then, his voice soft in defeat, he added, "I did what you wanted. I told him we were done."

"It's for the best, you know. You wouldn't have been happy with him. I'm the only one who can really make you soar."

Taylor's stomach rolled, and he could feel the bile rising up in his throat.

"I'm going to pick you up, Taylor, and I'm going to bring you back to my house. We're going to have so much fun together."

"Fine. Whatever."

Kevin laughed. It sounded eerie and hollow. "I know it'll take some time, Taylor, but you'll see just how perfect we are together. I promise it's going to be great. Meet me at the bus stop near your house in fifteen minutes."

Kevin made a kissing noise and hung up. Taylor changed out of his school clothes, throwing on a ratty T-shirt and jeans, and trudged to the bus stop. Kevin pulled up, leaned over, and opened the door. "Get in," he demanded.

Taylor slid into the seat and buckled the seat belt.

"You look great, babe. As always." Kevin leered.

"Why are you doing this, Kevin? Why can't you just leave me alone? Leave *us* alone?" he asked softly.

Kevin's voice turned harsh. "The only *us* from now on is me and you. Don't forget that. As for why? Pretty sure you know. I love you and I want you. I've wanted you since I first saw you. And no matter what you say, I know you feel the same way. I can tell by the way you looked at me, could tell by the way we kissed. You're a great kisser, you know that, right?"

Taylor turned his head away. He flinched when Kevin reached out and touched his knee.

"Don't worry, baby," he said softly. "I'm gonna make it all better for you. I promise."

DESPITE several attempts, Taylor refused to speak to his tormentor on the ride back to Kevin's house. When they got there, he grimaced as Kevin grabbed him by the hand and dragged him to the door.

"If my parents are home and they ask, you're with me now. Tell them we had a misunderstanding, but we worked it out. Say anything else, and Jackson won't be such a pretty boy anymore," Kevin snarled.

Taylor swallowed hard. It was the first direct threat Kevin had made, and Taylor's skin began to crawl. Fortunately Kevin's parents weren't home yet. Taylor grudgingly went to Kevin's bedroom, refusing to look anywhere but at his own feet. Upon entering the room, Kevin shut the door behind them and took off his jacket. He stepped over and began to unzip Taylor's.

Retreating several steps, Taylor said, "I can do it," and removed the outerwear.

Kevin moved in close and locked his hands around Taylor's neck, pulling him in tight. He kissed Taylor, his tongue insisting on entry. Taylor stood still, refusing any kind of reaction.

Kevin pulled back and glared at him. "Open your goddamn mouth, Taylor."

Kevin kissed him roughly, tongue probing against Taylor's lips. When Taylor's lips parted Kevin thrust in and began licking Taylor's teeth. Nausea flared, and Taylor jerked away, running to the en suite bathroom. He put his head over the toilet and convulsed harshly. Kevin stood dispassionately behind him.

Kevin leaned against the frame of the bathroom door, scowling at Taylor. "You're not making a good impression, Taylor. You realize that, right?"

Taylor took a few deep breaths and waited until his stomach settled, then moved to the sink, refusing to look at Kevin, and rinsed his mouth.

"Maybe it was too soon, Taylor," Kevin said, his voice heavy with sarcasm. "I can get that. Don't worry, though, we have time. We have all the time in the world."

"TAYLOR, honey, what's wrong? You've been so different these last couple of days."

"Nothing, Mom. It's fine."

"Is it Jackson? Is everything okay?"

Taylor gripped the table. "Not every goddamn thing is about Jackson, Mom. Just leave it alone, okay?" he bellowed.

He grabbed his lunch and stormed out the door, leaving his mother stunned and speechless.

All he wanted to do was go to homeroom and bury himself in a book, but the moment he walked into school, he heard his best friend calling out to him.

"Hey, Tay. What's going on? How are you?"

Taylor grimaced. He didn't want to do this. Not now. Not again. "I'm fine, Benny."

"Yeah? You don't seem it. Talk to me, please? Let me in." Benny placed his hand on Taylor's shoulder.

Taylor wanted so badly to talk to Benny. He needed his friend to understand. He needed his advice. He needed the comfort. He knew it was only a matter of time before Benny would wear him down, make him reveal what was wrong. He'd confront Kevin and might end up getting hurt. Kevin was dangerous, and Taylor knew what he had to do to keep his family safe.

Taylor shrugged off the hand. "What the hell, Benny? Why are you so freaking touchy-feely all the time? Just back off, would ya? God, you're always so damn needy. I... you know what, just... I don't want to talk to you, Benny. Maybe it'd be a good thing if we just cooled it, okay?"

Benny looked like he'd been slapped. "Taylor? What's this about? You're my bestie, Tay. I need...."

The anguish on Taylor's face was genuine. It was hurting him to talk to his friend this way. Still there wasn't a choice. "Why is it always about you, Benny? Huh? Why? Everything in the world revolves around Benny, is that it? Well, newsflash, buddy, it doesn't."

Benny peered at Taylor, his eyes wide. "Okay, Tay. I get it. I won't bother you anymore. Sorry."

As Benny shuffled away, Taylor knew he was going to be sick. He fled to the boy's bathroom and alternated between crying and being violently ill. He'd lost his boyfriend and his best friend and alienated his mother. He realized Kevin was systematically stripping everything from him. There wasn't a choice, though. He knew with all certainty if he defied Kevin, no one would be safe, and he had to separate himself from those he loved.

That night he was at Kevin's house. Kevin hadn't tried to kiss him again since that day, but he would still touch him. Sometimes intimately. Taylor swore his gooseflesh would never go away.

Taylor pulled open the front door of the house, eager for Kevin to take him home. He hated Kevin for what he was doing, but he hated himself more because he couldn't think of a way to stop it. When he saw the headlights pulling into the drive, his heart leapt into his throat. "My parents," Kevin hissed. He gripped Taylor tightly by the arm, pulled him close, hissing in his ear, "You don't say anything unless I tell you to, do you understand me?" He squeezed sharply on the muscle to emphasize what he said. Taylor nodded numbly.

"Kevin? Who's this?" Kevin's mother asked cautiously.

"Oh, that's right, you never met Taylor. Mom, Dad, this is Taylor. Taylor, this is my mom and dad," Kevin said brightly. He turned back to his parents, and his look sobered. "You remember that… incident we had a while back? It took some doing, but we finally got our problems worked out, and now we're back together."

Taylor's stomach clenched. He knew Kevin's parents would never believe it. He could see the doubt in their eyes. When Kevin wrapped an arm around Taylor's waist and pulled him close, it was all he could do to not scream.

"Well, Taylor, we're very glad we got the chance to meet you. Kevin was so upset over the problems you boys had. And then there was that awful bashing. Can you believe someone could hurt Kevin like that?"

Taylor suppressed a laugh, remembering Jackson telling him what happened. He simply shook his head and said, "No, ma'am."

"Yeah, Mom, it wasn't easy to convince Taylor of my good intentions. He was right, though, because he shouldn't take me back if he couldn't be sure about me and what I was capable of. That's why I love him, because he thinks with his heart as well as his head."

Taylor let out a small gasp as Kevin's fingers dug painfully into his side.

Kevin's father cleared his throat. For a brief moment Taylor thought his salvation was at hand. Surely this man would see how uncomfortable he was.

"C'mon, Adele, we should get inside and let the boys go on with what they're doing."

He led his wife into the house, leaving Taylor alone with Kevin. Without a word Taylor went to the car, buckled in, and slumped in the seat. His hopes crushed, it was all he could do to hold back the tears. Kevin got in and patted Taylor on the knee, saying, "I think my parents like you."

As much as he wished otherwise, Taylor couldn't stop the tears that slid down his cheeks.

He ran straight to his bedroom when he got home, wanting to avoid his parents, and stepped into the shower. He turned the water on as hot as it would go and scrubbed at his skin until it turned crimson. No matter how much he scoured it, he never felt clean. Tiny rivulets of blood formed at the points where he perforated the skin from the constant abrasions. He watched in fascination as the water turned pink and drained away. He'd tried so hard to be strong. To protect his family. Here, though, in his bathroom, alone, he felt small and helpless. He curled up on the floor of the bathtub and sobbed as the water continued to pour down on him, washing away all evidence of his shame.

CHAPTER TWELVE
REVENGE

IT HAD been a week since he'd seen Jackson. Taylor's gut flared every homeroom, waiting for his boyfriend to walk in, but Jackson never did. Taylor was frantic with worry but didn't dare to ask any questions. Kevin had Taylor's day all planned out, and he was too afraid to deviate from the schedule. Taylor became more withdrawn. He didn't speak with anyone at school. Each class bled into the next. He drifted through the day, unsure of where he was or where he was supposed to be. Each night he was at Kevin's. The touching had gradually grown to include small kisses on the face and eyes. Each time Kevin would touch him, though, Taylor would flinch or draw away. Kevin was growing increasingly frustrated with him.

"What the hell, Taylor? It's like you don't love me," he spat.

Taylor's eyes blazed, but he didn't speak.

"Look, Taylor," Kevin cooed softly, "It's all right. Really. Just let it happen. You'll enjoy it again, I know you will." He ran his fingers lightly over Taylor's cheek, then bent in and kissed him softly on the lips. Taylor closed his eyes and began to lean into the kiss. Kevin's fingers tightened sharply on the back of Taylor's neck, dragging him deeper into the kiss. Images of Jackson flashed through Taylor's mind, the final one of Jackson's shattered look forced him to scramble away from Kevin.

"No," he gasped, "I don't want you."

"Goddamn it, Taylor," Kevin shouted When he raised his hand, Taylor turned his head and waited for the blow. "No, not like this. Get dressed, Taylor. I'm taking you home."

"Home?" Taylor whined pitifully.

"Yes, baby. I'm taking you home. Get ready so we can leave, okay?"

Taylor nearly bounced across the room to grab his jacket and ran to the car, eager to leave, to go home, and try again to scrub himself clean.

Kevin neared the bus stop where he would drop Taylor off and reached across the seat, stroked Taylor's leg, and announced, "I know why this is so hard, Taylor. I'm really sorry I didn't realize it before. I promise I'm going to fix it, though. You'll see. We *will* be happy."

Taylor stepped out and was about to bolt from the car when a voice brought him up short. "Tay? What the hell? What are you doing?"

Taylor was rooted to the spot. His brain was screaming *run*, but his feet refused to move.

"Taylor, I asked you a question. What are you doing with... *him?*" Benny spat.

Kevin slowly moved out of the car, drew himself up to his full height, and glared at Benny.

"He's with me now. He's not any concern of yours."

"The hell he's not!" Benny roared. He charged at Kevin until Taylor's cry brought him up short. "No, Benny, don't. It's true."

Benny stopped, looking dazed. "What are you saying? What's going on?" Benny demanded.

"I... love him, Benny. He makes me happy. Can't you just be happy for me? You were my best friend once. Please?"

The look on Benny's face pierced Taylor's heart. Defeated. Dazed. Nauseous. He couldn't be certain what emotions were playing over the normally cheerful demeanor.

"This doesn't wash, Taylor. I know you're upset about Jackson, but this isn't right," Benny stuttered.

"I broke up with Jackson so I could be with Kevin. I *want* to be with Kevin," he tried to say with conviction, but he knew it would take more than words to convince his friend.

Taylor strode over to where Kevin stood and purposefully placed a kiss on his cheek. Kevin turned into the kiss and claimed Taylor, consuming his mouth. Pulling away, Kevin whispered in Taylor's ear, "Good job, babe." Taylor hoped he could hide the disgust he felt as he turned to face Benny. Anger radiated off his friend, his face twisted into a bizarre mask.

"You... we... no, this is wrong, Taylor," he said angrily. "I can't believe you're doing this after everything *he* did."

Benny stormed away and tears dotted Taylor's cheeks. Kevin traced his fingers lightly over the tears, smoothing them into the warm skin.

Kevin put his hand on Taylor's hip and gave a sick smile. "That was really very good, Taylor. I knew you'd get into it eventually. I promise it's going to be a lot easier now. I'll see you tomorrow."

Kevin kissed Taylor on the cheek and stroked his hair before getting back into the car and driving away. That night there wasn't enough hot water or mouthwash in the house to make him feel clean. Even after he scrubbed his skin raw, Taylor hoped it couldn't get any worse than it was.

TAYLOR found sleep wasn't going to come easily. He lay in bed tossing and turning for several hours before he finally drifted off. He could hear a buzzing in the distance. The sound was irritating. And loud. It took a few moments to register that his phone was ringing. Taylor scrambled to pick it up. Three thirty in the morning. Who the hell would be calling?

"What?" he growled into the phone.

"Taylor?" a soft voice gasped. "Taylor, is it you? It's Becca."

Taylor bolted upright. "Becca? What do you want? Why are you calling?"

Becca began sobbing uncontrollably, and Taylor found it hard to understand her as she tried to speak. "Mr. Kern called me," she sobbed. "I'm the only friend of Jackson's he knows. I said I'd call the others. He… he… oh God…. They don't know…."

A cold, hard knot formed in Taylor's stomach. "Becca, please, what are you saying?" he pleaded.

"There was… an accident. They don't know if…."

"Jackson…," Taylor moaned pitifully. *Please no, not Jackson.*

"He's hurt. It's bad. Really bad. They don't know if…." She hesitated. Taylor didn't need to hear any more. He knew what her next words were going to be. "They're just not sure," she said finally.

He was numb. He wanted to ask, but he didn't really want to know. "What happened, Becca?" he said, barely a whisper.

"It was a hit and run. Someone ran him down and left him lying by the side of the road."

Taylor's blood ran cold, and his mouth opened in a noiseless scream. His phone fell to the floor. He threw the lamp across the room, the glass shattering against the far wall. He wailed as he began pulling things from the shelves and smashing them to pieces. The mirror on his bureau became razor sharp shards, strewn across the room when he threw a chair through it. His father dashed into the room and immediately threw himself onto Taylor, who flailed and fought against him.

"Get off! I need to go. Dad, please! Get off," he cried out.

"Taylor, what's wrong? What's going on? Talk to me, son, please!"

Taylor could barely get the words out. He was having a hard time catching his breath. "It's Jackson. He's… hurt. Dying, maybe. I have to go."

"What? I'll drive you. Let me grab some clothes. Just wait here."

After his dad was out of the room, Taylor threw on some clothes, grabbed his phone and the keys, and ran to the car. He threw it into gear and sped away.

TAYLOR stopped the car in front of Kevin's house and rushed to the door. He began pounding on it, demanding entrance. Kevin opened the door, sleep heavy in his eyes.

"Taylor? What the hell, babe? Why are you here?"

"Your car. Show me your car!" he said harshly.

"What are you—"

"Show me your goddamn car, Kevin!" he shrieked.

He grabbed Kevin and dragged him to the garage, throwing him against the door.

"Open it. Now," he demanded.

When Kevin turned the key in the lock, Taylor pushed past him and inspected the front of the Hyundai. A smashed lens cap and crushed bumper told him everything he needed to know. He spun on Kevin.

"What did you do? Why, Kevin? I did what you asked. Why did you hurt him?"

Kevin's smile was predatory. He stalked toward Taylor. "He was in the way, Taylor. You weren't giving yourself to me, even though I knew you wanted to. I knew it was because of *him*. I drove past his house. It really wasn't hard to find. The Internet is an amazing thing. He was out running when I got there. It was a lot easier than I thought it would be. I just waited until he was far enough away from anyone, gunned the engine and.... Well, I guess I don't need to be graphic."

"You son of a bitch!" Taylor screamed.

Kevin continued to advance on him. Taylor backed off slightly, staring daggers at the person responsible for the tragedy.

"I did what you wanted. I gave you what you asked for. Jackson was out of my life. You didn't need to do it," he wailed, tucking his arms in and rocking in place.

"You're wrong, love. So wrong," Kevin hissed. He grabbed Taylor by the shoulders and drew him close. "This just proves now that you're mine. With Jackson being dead, you don't have anything else to go back to. Now it's just you and me, the way it should be."

Taylor pushed Kevin back and laughed harshly. "He's not dead. He's in the hospital, but you didn't win. I love Jackson and could never, will never, love you," he snarled, eyes blazing with fury.

Kevin backhanded Taylor across the face, causing Taylor to crumple to the floor. He got back to his feet unsteadily, blood oozing from the split in his lip.

"You know the old saying, right? If at first you don't succeed. Don't worry, I made you a promise that I'd make everything better. It shouldn't be too hard to get to Jackson." Kevin grinned, chuckling maniacally.

Taylor's eyes darkened. He could feel his blood boiling. He wailed and threw himself onto Kevin, latching fingers around his throat. Kevin clawed at Taylor's hands, trying to push him off, but Taylor refused to be budged. He squeezed, feeling his fury wash over him. Kevin's eyes bulged, and his face went ashen. His head dropped back, his body went limp, and suddenly he was still. Taylor let go and stepped back as Kevin fell to the floor. Then he calmly reached into his pocket, extracted his phone, and dialed.

"911, please state the nature of your emergency."

"I think he's dead. I killed him."

PITCH

CHAPTER THIRTEEN
AFTERMATH

AS THE alarms drew closer, Taylor sat down next to Kevin's body and waited. His rage diminished, he sat in stunned silence over his act of violence. Taylor looked up from where he was sitting, head in his hands as the police entered the garage guns drawn. "Don't move," one of the officers called out. They didn't need to worry. Taylor sat passively as they pulled his hands behind him, and he felt the cold steel of the cuffs being snapped into place around his wrists.

As Taylor looked on, one of the officers pressed his fingers to Kevin's neck, turned, and called out to a colleague. "He's alive. Get the paramedics in here, now!"

Another of the officers knelt next to Taylor and asked, "Son, can you tell us what happened?"

"I killed him. I choked him to death," Taylor gasped out. He looked down at his feet, but his eyes were unfocused, his breath coming in ragged gasps.

"He's still alive. What happened?" the officer asked again.

Taylor tried to look up, but his head was spinning. "He… he ran Jackson down. He laughed about it." Taylor could feel the sweat soaking his shirt. "He didn't have to do it. I did what he asked. I let him touch me, kiss me…. I didn't want to, but he said he'd hurt Jackson. I did everything he told me and even after that, he still tried to take him away from me. Why did he do it?" Taylor sobbed.

"This kid might be in shock," said one of the entering paramedics. "Let me check him over."

They pushed Taylor down onto the floor, propped up his feet, and covered him with a blanket. The paramedics were checking his vital signs when Taylor's cell phone rang, startling him. It was his mom's ring tone.

"Mom," he cried out, closing his eyes tightly.

The officer picked up the phone and opened it. Taylor heard her voice, so far away and garbled.

"Your folks are going to meet you at the hospital, kid. The paramedics want to get you checked out before we talk, okay?"

Taylor nodded numbly.

TAYLOR'S head felt like it was going to burst when they put him into the ambulance. The paramedics tried to talk with him, but he couldn't focus on what they were saying. His head was spinning, and he couldn't collect his thoughts. He could see the lights flashing outside the window, and the siren blared loudly, but in the moment they were a jumble with little meaning.

The next thing he was aware of was his mother's hand on his face—her voice seemed to come from so far away. "Taylor? Honey, we're here. It's going to be okay." He shook his head harshly. Nothing was going to be okay again. He was going to lose everything he loved.

After checking him over, the doctor smiled and told Taylor he needed to rest and assured him he'd be okay after he slept for a while. They moved Taylor to a room, his parents still by his side. The last thing he remembered was his mother smiling down at him as he drifted off.

Sunlight streaming into the room woke Taylor. He shut his eyes tightly, trying to block out the glare. "Dad, can you close the curtains, please?" he asked.

"Sure, Taylor, just give me a minute."

He heard his dad move across the room and heard the shades being drawn, darkening the room. A knock at the door startled him. He looked over as an older police officer entered the room.

"Mr. And Mrs. Andrews, I'm Officer Lawson," he said, shaking Taylor's parents' hands. "I know this isn't a good time, but

I'm going to need to talk to Taylor. He turned to Taylor. "Mr. Andrews, you are under arrest for the assault on Kevin Richardson."

Taylor squeezed his eyes shut and drew his knees to his chest, rocking slowly. "No, please no, I can't... I can't do this, please don't let this happen," he cried softly.

Taylor's dad leapt out of the chair. "That punk hurt my son," he shouted. "He could have killed the other boy. How the hell can you arrest him for protecting his friend?"

"Sir, I'm doing my job. It's not up to me to decide his guilt or innocence. Taylor, you have the right to remain silent. Anything you say can and will be used against you in a court of law. You have the right to speak to an attorney. If you want one but cannot afford it, one will be appointed to you. Do you understand these rights as I've read them to you?"

"Yes, sir. I'm sorry about this." Taylor couldn't think of anything else to say.

"I need to know what happened," the officer said blandly. He looked at Taylor, and his features softened. "The boy's fine. He's going to be hurting for a while, but he'll be okay."

Taylor inhaled deeply. At least he hadn't killed anyone. He began to recount the week, talking about how Kevin had phoned him, threatened Jackson, forced Taylor to come to him, touched him and, finally, how he found out Kevin had run Jackson down. The officer made notes, asked a few more questions, then explained to Taylor he and his parents or his counsel would need to come to the station after he was released, and then left.

"Mom," Taylor asked hesitantly, "did Jackson...?"

"No, Taylor. Jackson's okay," she said gently. "He's strong and he's fighting. Everything is going to be all right."

"I wanted to kill Kevin, Mom," Taylor admitted, shocked by the hatred in his voice. "I wanted to hurt him for what he did to Jackson. For what he made *me* do to Jackson. If Jackson dies, he's never going to know, Mom. He's never going to know I love him." Tears leaked down the side of Taylor's face. He wiped them with the corner of the blanket.

Taylor sniffed a couple of times, trying to hold back more tears. His mother pulled him into a tight hug. "It's going to be okay, Taylor. I promise," she murmured in his ear, rocking him gently.

A cold shudder ran through Taylor's body. "No, Mom, it's not going to be okay," he whispered. He looked up and grabbed her hands. "Jackson's in the hospital because I messed up again. And because of it, I'm going to have to go to jail."

"We've talked with Ellen Patterson. She's a lawyer, and she's going to see what she can do to get you home with us. I wish I could make it better, honey. I know it hurts bad, but we're going to get through this."

She sat at the edge of the bed and pulled him into another hug. It was then that Taylor's unavoidable explosion of tears came.

Ms. Patterson arranged it so Taylor would be released to his parent's custody upon his discharge from the hospital. He was allowed to go home late the second day. His parents basically kept him under house arrest, telling him that after everything he'd been through, he needed rest and that the doctors had agreed with them.

Taylor sat at his desk, trying to concentrate on the book he was reading. *Plan B* was a new book written by one of his favorite authors, SJD Peterson. He knew from the reviews that it was a great book, but he just couldn't focus on it. He sighed and powered down the Nook, placing it back on the shelf. When the phone rang, he glanced at it fretfully. After all the problems he'd had, it was the phone that still made him nervous. When he saw Becca's number, he sighed. "Hello, Becca, what do you need?" he asked sharply.

"Hi, Taylor," she replied nervously. "I just wanted to let you know that I spoke with Mr. Kern. He called to tell me that they think Jackson is going to recover. They think there might be some kind of residual damage, but they don't know how bad it's going to be."

Taylor sucked in a deep breath. At least Jackson was going to be okay.

"I wanted to say I'm sorry too. I know it won't change anything, but I need you to know why I acted like I did. I was so jealous, Taylor. He had everything, and I wanted that. The thing he didn't want was me. He had confided in me how much he wanted to get to know you better. He said he thought you were *intriguing*. I messed up badly, Taylor. I don't expect you'll ever forgive me, and I don't deserve it, but I am so, so sorry."

"Becca, I really don't want to talk to you right now, okay?" Taylor said good-bye and disconnected. He didn't want to talk to her about this now. Not while the wounds were still raw.

The one thing Taylor regretted most was the fact Benny wouldn't return his calls. He'd tried several times to get in contact with him. He needed his best friend. Each time he spoke with Benny's parents, they told him the same thing: Benny was unavailable to speak, and they would give him the message, but he never called back.

TAYLOR'S parents took him to see Ms. Patterson. They were ushered into the meeting room and asked to take a seat around the large oval table. Taylor sat in one of the heavy leather chairs, drumming his fingers on the tabletop, while his eyes darted around the room taking in all the volumes of law books on the shelves. The door swung open, and his father stood to greet the woman who entered.

"Ms. Patterson, thank you for your call."

"Thank you all for coming down," she said, turning her gaze to Taylor. "How are you holding up, Taylor?"

Taylor looked down at his fingers, not able to look her in the eye.

"I'm okay," he replied. "I really want to get out of the house."

"I know. We just thought it would be better if you stayed at home for a while. I do have some news, though. I spoke with the District Attorney's office. They aren't going to pursue charges in your case. The evidence against Kevin Richards shows he'd been stalking both you and Jackson. He had quite a collection of pictures of the two of you stashed in his bedroom."

Taylor shuddered. The thought of Kevin having pictures of him and Jackson disgusted him.

"The police matched the damage done to Kevin's car to the accident, proof that he was the one who hit Jackson. Kevin is also being very vocal. He blames everything on Jackson, saying that if Jackson hadn't come between you and him, you would have come back to him."

Taylor's head snapped up.

"That's a lie!" Taylor shouted. "I was never with Kevin, not the way he wanted. I went out with him once and that... ended badly," he admitted, his voice trailing off.

"Yes, we know. The police investigated when Kevin's parents called about their son being beaten up. Kevin admitted he hit you, but when you didn't press charges they let it drop."

"This is my fault," Taylor whispered, eyes moving back to his hands.

"No, it's not. Kevin's a sick person. There was no way you could have known what was going to happen. Yes, it would have been best if you had come forward, but that doesn't mean it would have changed anything at all. Kevin probably still would have found a way to blame you and gone ahead with what he did. Regardless, the DA doesn't think they'd be able to pursue the case and get a judgment, so they're going to drop the charges against you. You're still going to have to appear in court to testify against Kevin when his case comes up. You're still going to have to face him. Do you understand?"

Taylor nodded. "I know." He looked up and met Ms. Patterson's eyes for the first time. "Thank you for this."

"You're welcome," she responded with a warm smile.

"Can I go and see Jackson now?" he asked hopefully.

"As long as it's okay with your parents, yes."

Taylor's heart pounded heavily. It had been two weeks, and he was afraid. He felt like he had hurt so many people so badly; he wasn't sure if he could face them. His mother had tried to assure him he hadn't done anything wrong. He'd tried to do what he thought was necessary to protect his friends, but on some level, he couldn't help but blame himself for what had happened to Jackson.

"He needs to hear from you, Taylor," his mom said softly. "I don't know if he will be able to move past it, but he needs to know why, and it should come from you. You'll regret it if you don't try."

Taylor knew she was right. If he didn't at least tell Jackson how sorry he was, he could never forgive himself, no matter if it meant he'd lose Jackson anyway.

TAYLOR caught his first glimpse of Jackson from the door of the hospital room, and it took his breath away. Jackson looked frightening. So many bruises. Casts covered his lower body and right arm, his face was puffy and swollen, mottled in different dark shades of red, blue, and purple. He had so many tubes and patches across his arms and chest, each monitoring different functions. It made him look artificial, and the soft beeps and whirs from the machines, a steady sound in the background, added to the illusion. Taylor gasped, and his heart ached when he saw his beautiful man that way. He tiptoed quietly into the room and sat down, folded his arms on the bed, and laid his head across them.

"Hi, Jackson," he began, "it's me. I don't know if you can hear me, and I know I'm probably the last person you want to see, but I wanted to tell you how sorry I am about everything that happened. I need you to understand that I didn't want to break up with you. I love you so much. I had just found you, you know? I was really looking forward to seeing what life had in store for us. I wanted it all, Jackson," Taylor lamented. "I had you, my very best friend, some great parents, and Kevin stripped them away from me. He took everything, Jackson. Everything I loved, he tore it away. I was so scared he would hurt you or Benny or someone else I cared about. I couldn't see any other choice. And I'm so goddamn sorry."

Taylor sobbed out the words, begging for forgiveness from everyone for what he'd done, because no matter what else, all the pain was his fault. He'd been the one who pushed them away.

"I hurt you so bad. I hurt Benny. And I know neither one of you will ever look at me the same way again. The smile in your eyes will go to someone else. Benny's goodness will turn to some new person. And I deserve it. I know that. I don't deserve either one of you," he sobbed, tears blurring his vision.

"You know you're an idiot, right, Tay?" a soft voice called from the doorway.

Taylor's head jerked up. "Benny?" he cried. He wanted to run to his friend and hold him, but he remained frozen to the chair, unsure. Benny looked haggard. His eyes had dark circles, his hair looked unkempt, and he seemed pale and drawn.

Before Benny dropped his gaze to the floor, Taylor saw the pain in his friend's eyes. "Why couldn't you talk to me? I would have helped you. It hurt so badly when I saw you with him. When you said you loved him. It hurt, Tay," Benny wheezed. "I couldn't call you back. I was afraid of what you might say. I'm sorry I let you down."

The tears streaming down Benny's face matched his own. Neither of them moved.

"Benny, I'm sorry. I thought I had to protect you all. He threatened to hurt people. He *did* hurt people. And it's all my fault. I know I don't deserve a friend like you."

Taylor sat in the chair, refusing to look up. He didn't dare look Benny in the face. He couldn't stand to see the hurt or anger in his friend's eyes. He heard feet shuffling before he felt Benny's muscular arms encircle him tightly. He stood and buried his face in Benny's shoulder, crushing him in a desperate embrace, afraid if he loosened it, even for just a moment, he'd lose his friend again.

"God, Benny, I'm so *so* sorry. I screwed up so bad. It hurts, Benny. I needed you so much, and I couldn't... I didn't...." He gasped for breath. Benny's hands were warm, rubbing circles around his back.

"Let it out, Tay. It's okay, I've got you. Just let it out," Benny said in a subdued voice.

Taylor pulled back, moving a distance away from his friend. "No, I can't. I don't deserve it. I don't deserve any of it," he cried out, scrambling farther out of Benny's reach.

Benny held out his arms, but didn't move. "Tay, come here," he said in a calm voice.

Taylor took a hesitant step.

"Come on, get back in here." Benny smiled. "It's okay, Taylor. It's where you need to be right now. It's where I need you to be. You need your best friend, don't you?"

And with those words, Taylor's facade cracked. Sobbing convulsively, he launched himself at Benny, who snatched him up in big, strong arms and held him close while Taylor let out all the hurt and frustration.

"Why, Benny? Why are you doing this?"

Benny put his lips next to Taylor's ear and said softly, but very firmly, "Because, you idiot, you're my best friend. I love you. You're hurting, and that makes me hurt."

Taylor let Benny's words soothe him, let Benny hold him until he was able to calm down. Finally, when he had better control, he extracted himself from Benny and looked at him curiously. "Benny, why are you here?"

Benny blushed slightly. "I've been coming every day, Tay. I didn't understand why you weren't coming, and I didn't want him to be alone, so I sit with Jackson, talk to him. I tell him stuff about what's going on. Becca comes in once in a while, and we talk with him together. She's pretty broken up. She's asked him to forgive her so many times. I keep telling her I'm sure he will, but she always looks so shattered when she leaves. I know she blames herself too."

"She shouldn't. This isn't her fault at all. It's all mine. I was stupid, and it should have been.... Oh my God, Benny, it should have just been me! Kevin loved me, so he didn't—"

"Stop please! Just stop," Benny hissed. "Kevin didn't love you. He was obsessed with you, yes, but there was never love. He wanted to control you. He wanted that power. But he never, *ever* loved you. Not like Jackson does. Not like I do. He's sick, Tay. He's sick and he needs help."

Taylor sniffed, wiped his sleeve across his nose, and went back over to Jackson's bedside. He brushed a lock of hair off

Jackson's forehead and placed a gentle kiss where it had lain. He took Jackson's hand in his, lightly tracing slow, small, gentle circles across the back of it, careful of the IV tubes. Benny stepped behind Taylor and began to rub his shoulders. Taylor slumped in the chair as the tension began to melt away. The fear remained, however, and he knew Benny could see it on him.

"He's going to be okay, Taylor. It's all going to be okay," Benny said in a soothing voice. "He's a strong guy. He's going to be fine, and he's going to come back to you."

But Taylor knew Benny couldn't make that promise, no matter how much he wished otherwise. They sat there, talking with Jackson, until visiting hours ended and then made their way to the parking garage.

Taylor stood awkwardly, fingers pulling at a string on his jacket. "Thank you for coming to see him," he said quietly. "I was so worried about him being alone, but knowing you were there for him—"

"I wanted to be there for both of you. Jackson was... is important to you, and that makes him important to me."

Taylor gave a weak smile. He could see Benny was just as uncomfortable as he was. In all the years they had been friends, they'd never been so nervous around each other. He reached out and grabbed Benny's coat and pulled him into a close hug.

"You're one of the most amazing people ever, you know that, right?"

Benny chuckled. "Of course I do. Who do you think has been telling you that for years?"

They clung to each other tightly. The discomfort wasn't completely gone, but Taylor knew they'd be okay in time.

Taylor lay in bed that night, hoping to find some kind of peace, but it eluded him. He thought about it for a while and realized he had to make the peace on his own. He pulled his phone out and dialed the number.

"Hi, Becca. Can we talk?"

CHAPTER FOURTEEN
PERSPECTIVE

TAYLOR lay back on the bed, making himself as comfortable as he could.

"Sure, Taylor. What did you want to talk about?" Becca asked, a hint of suspicion evident in her voice.

"I know this might sound kind of weird, but I want you to tell me about Jackson, you know, during the time you—"

"I'm sorry, Taylor. Really." Her voice broke. "I know you hate me, and I don't blame you."

"No, that's not why I'm asking," Taylor soothed. "I just want to know things, small things I might have missed. I was hoping you could fill in some of the gaps for me." There was silence for a moment. "Please?"

She breathed a heavy sigh and hesitantly began telling her story. "When he walked into the classroom for the first time, I was floored," she began. "He was one of the hottest guys I'd ever seen. I fell for his eyes. It was kind of weird. I've had a lot of boyfriends, but none of them ever made me... tingle. His voice was so sexy. When Mrs. Wagner asked for someone to show him around, I jumped at the chance. He came over and sat down next to me, and I felt like I could just melt. We just talked for the period, and I knew I had to have him. Especially when I found out he was going to play baseball. That seriously amped his status for me."

Taylor shook his head. Of course, it was about status for her.

"After the bell rang, I grabbed him by the arm and we started heading out of class. I chatted away, but I noticed he didn't really look at me. His eyes wandered all around. I just figured it was because he was new. Over the next few days, we got pretty comfortable talking to one another. He was witty and engaging, a real charmer. I fell hard."

Taylor remembered that first day. He could understand why Becca would fall for Jackson. Probably the same reason he did. He wasn't sure why it was so important to talk to her, but he needed it. He needed those missing pieces of time that were taken from him, and Becca was the only one who could fill those gaps.

"The day of the baseball tryouts was pretty intense. I had no idea he was so good at the game. Watching him pitch thrilled me. I'd never seen anyone so amazing. I've dated baseball players before, but Jax was unique. When the coach told Jax he had a spot, I just flew across the field and threw my arms around him. I thought it was pretty strange because he only gave me a quick squeeze. I wasn't used to not having a guy's attention, but I kept thinking he was just excited about the team. That never changed, though. Jax was always looking for something. I never knew what it was, but that didn't mean I stopped trying to get him to look at me. A couple of weeks into practice, though, he came over and pulled me aside and asked me who the blond guy with the curly hair was. I looked over and saw you and told him who you were. I asked why he was wondering, and he just smiled and said he thought you were intriguing. He was enjoying watching you sketch something in your book."

Taylor smiled so wide his cheeks hurt. Even though Becca was telling the story, he swore he could hear Jackson's voice in his head.

"It took another week for him to tell me he thought you were cute," she said resignedly. "Then I knew why he wasn't interested in me, and I felt stupid. I was angry with you because I thought... I don't know... I thought you were stealing him away from me, even though he was never mine to begin with. He wanted to talk to you, but I kept distracting him. When you would come up to him in class, I needed to be sure you didn't get close to him. I was very careful not to let you in, Taylor," she said, her voice soft. "After the first game, he was a megastar, and I admit I enjoyed being on his coattails. In class that day, everyone was coming up to him and talking to him about how great he was. Then you walked by and said something. I'm not sure what it was, and you just kept going. He called after you, but you didn't stop. I remember the look on his face. He was so disappointed. He had the whole school after him, and you were the one he saw. It was at that point that I started to hate you."

Her bluntness shocked Taylor, but he wanted her to continue. Her words were soothing to him, even if they were hard to hear.

"I went to the tournament in Beloit to watch him play but also to keep an eye on him. I was stupid, I know, but I figured if I could keep the two of you apart, then maybe Jax would notice me. The game wasn't going well. His pitching was really awful in the early innings. Only some really great plays by the other guys kept them close in the game. Jax would come over to the dugout and pace. He kept mumbling to himself like he was upset about something, but I didn't know about what at the time. In the seventh inning he went back out to the mound, and suddenly he seemed relaxed. That was where he started acknowledging the crowd, or at least that's what I thought he was doing. After the inning, he bowed. It was so dorky I had to laugh. He ran back to the dugout, came over to me, and whispered, '*He's here!*' and just like that everything was good for him again. I looked into the stands, and I saw you there, and I knew he had seen you."

Taylor's heart swelled. He remembered Jackson telling him this, but to know that Jackson had told others filled him with warmth.

"After the game was over, he hurried over to me and asked if I knew where you'd gone. He'd hoped to catch you so the two of you could talk. I didn't know where you were and said so. He didn't look happy. When we left the game, I tried to comfort him, but he wasn't at all interested. We got back to the school, and he headed straight for his truck and left. It wasn't until the next day he told me he'd talked to some people and found out where you lived. He went to your house to talk to you, but apparently you weren't home."

149

Taylor sighed. "Yeah, Becca, I was. I saw him through the window, and I got so freaked out he was there I didn't know what to do. By the time Benny told me to talk to him, he had already left."

"He made you nervous too?" Becca chuckled. "Monday morning he came to school and you were all he talked about. I was all kinds of upset about it because I knew he liked you, and I wanted it to be me. I didn't want to give up what was fast becoming my ticket to the top. If I had known, Taylor…."

"You couldn't know, Becca. No one could. I know you were being selfish, but I don't think you were being malicious, at least, I hope not."

"Well…," she began slowly, "it didn't start out that way, but the more I saw how into you he was, the more jealous I became. I really didn't like you much at the time, and I got bitchier every time he would talk about you. He was crushing hard on you, Taylor, and I knew if you got together with him, I'd lose it all. I was angry about it, and that's when I did something stupid. You had come into class after that weekend, and I saw you heading over to Jax. I got angry and hurt and wanted to keep you away from him so I…."

Taylor remembered all too well what she'd done. Up until this month it had been one of the lowest points of his life.

"I'm sorry for what I did, Taylor. Jackson never once said anything bad about you. He acted like you hung the freaking moon and stars, and I wanted that, you know? I wanted someone to look at me like that. So I lied to both of you. I told you he thought you were disgusting and you should stay away. I told him I'd talk to you and find out what you thought of him. Then I went back and told him you weren't interested. He was hurt. I could see it in his face, but I couldn't stop myself from trying to hold on."

Taylor closed his eyes.

"He asked me if you were seeing Benny. I figured if he thought you were with someone, you'd be off limits to him or something, so I told him you were."

Taylor laughed. Him and Benny? Like *that* would ever happen.

"At the state finals he was really pumped. He was excited the team had made it to state and he was a part of it. What made it better for him, though, is he saw you there. Every time he'd smile and wave, it was his way of making sure you were there, to see that you were in the crowd. It got to the point where he *had* to see you, even if he would never do anything about it because he thought you were with someone," she said softly.

Taylor rubbed the back of his neck. He really didn't want to hear more, but he really needed it.

"When you were gone for the summer, it was really hard on him. He was moody and out of sorts all the time, pretty much kept to himself. I didn't see a lot of him the first couple of weeks. He took up running, said it was to burn off nervous energy. He used to laugh and say the runner's high made him feel better. After a while I started going running with him, to keep him company, I guess, but also to be able to spend time with him. He would talk about you on our runs. Wondering what you were doing, where you were, if you were with Benny. I was torn between telling him to shut up and telling him the truth. I pretty much stayed quiet, though."

It warmed Taylor to know Jackson thought about him while he was away. It was strange, but hearing Becca talk about Jackson made him feel less alone in his head. Jackson had told Taylor he'd thought about him, but when Becca told him, it was almost like he could feel it from Jackson's perspective.

"Everything started coming apart at the Halloween dance. I... you know I always put you at the refreshment table, right?"

Taylor chuckled. "Yeah, I kinda figured that out."

"I wanted you far away from where Jax would be. I figured out of sight, out of mind. But that didn't work out either. When Jackson got to the dance, he saw you at the table and started heading your way. I caught him and dragged him to the dance floor with me, but he wouldn't take his eyes off you. I was so angry, even though I knew in my head I didn't have the right to be. I... purposely tried to make you mad by touching him."

"It worked," Taylor said in a hushed voice.

"When Jackson saw that guy talking to you, he got hurt and angry. He was upset because he still thought you were with Benny and now this guy, but you wouldn't give him the time of day. He went home right after he saw you hand the guy your phone. He was pretty upset."

"I didn't know," Taylor mumbled, swallowing a painful lump in his throat. There was so much he wished he'd known, wanted to do over. Even knowing it wasn't intentional, it stung that he had hurt Jackson by making him think he wasn't good enough.

"That week I heard a lot of complaining. Jackson kept asking what was wrong with him that you wouldn't look at him or talk to him. He was hurting, and I was stupid because I took pleasure from his pain. I know it was selfish, but it gave me more time to be with him, to be his friend. Then you came into school with the black eye. I got bitchier and got snotty toward you. Jackson saw your face, and he freaked. I tried to keep him away from you, but he ignored me. He was determined he was going to talk to you. You shot him down, though, and stormed away. He was concerned about you and hurt that you wouldn't let him be there."

She sighed softly. "Taylor, do you really want me to continue? How does this change anything? Are you enjoying me confessing? Is that what this is?"

"No, Becca," Taylor said confidently. "You know what happened, right? You know I broke up with Jackson?"

"Yes," she said weakly. "Benny told me."

"I didn't want to do it—" Taylor started, then decided he didn't want to let her into his life like that. "Something happened and everything got so messed up. Now I'm afraid Jackson is going to hate me. I'm afraid I'm never going to have the chance to make things right. You're really the only connection I have to him, and I need that right now. I need to hear the things you know. I just need to know how he feels… how he felt about me. Please continue."

He heard her sigh through the phone, and then she said, "When you came back with a black eye, I was so horrid to you. I said awful, disgusting things. Jax watched you. He told me he wanted to say something, but you had been so harsh to him, and he didn't know how to approach you. What he really wanted was to protect you, because he knew what was coming. He let it be known he wouldn't tolerate bullying. Everyone he talked to knew how Jax felt about picking on people, and they respected him enough to not do it, at least not in front of him. He did everything he could to make school less harsh on you. As much as I was hating you, I was so impressed by the fact he would stand with you, even when he was standing alone."

Taylor sniffled. He thought Jackson had something to do with why he didn't get much crap, but he never knew he'd gone out of his way to make it easier on him.

"When Jax started doing the community drives, he was head-over-heels happy with the fact you were going to help out. It became a big deal to him that it all succeeded because he wanted to make you proud of him. He wanted you to see him in a positive way, to get over what he thought were your true feelings about him. He was completely driven to earn your respect. He was constantly wondering what else he could do, what he should do, everything had to go right. It all had to be a big success. He was constantly trying to improve things, to make life better. And I felt guilty because I was only doing it for me."

"Becca, why are you doing this now? What's changed that we're talking? I thought you hated me?"

"I do. I did. I don't know, Taylor," she admitted, sounding frustrated. "Hearing what happened to Jackson, I realized if I hadn't been a bitch to you, maybe he could have been a happier person. Maybe he would have been able to find himself instead of trying to constantly prove himself to others."

She paused for a moment. Taylor waited, figuring she was trying to regain her composure before she continued.

"The accident… what happened scared me. It showed me how quickly everything could change. Jackson was on the top of the social ladder, and where did it get him?" She sniffed and blew her nose. "When I was sitting with him in the hospital, I was surprised more people from school didn't show up. A few here and there, but it was mostly just me and Benny. I kind of realized most people were phony. They'd be your best friends when you were a big shot, but when you weren't? It was time to move on. And I did that to a lot of people. I never realized how much it hurt to be that person," she said sadly.

Taylor felt some measure of sympathy for Becca, but he still didn't trust her. What she was saying, though, was the same thing Benny had told him about people not being Jackson's friends and how, if things went bad, they'd just abandon him.

"Anyway," she continued, "Christmas came around, and Jackson really wanted to give you something. He had found a sketchbook in a store, and he just had to have it for you. He dragged me along to see it and told me it was the perfect gift, and he just knew you'd love it. It cost him a pretty penny, but he didn't care. This was the gift he just *had* to buy. He thought about giving it to you directly, hoping it would be a chance for him to talk to you, but he didn't want to resort to bribery to do it, so he decided he was going to pass it through like a student council gift. He was so proud of that sketchbook, Taylor. He knew when you drew something it would be like a part of him was in that drawing, too."

Taylor smiled at the thought and cast a glance at the book on his nightstand. He thumbed through the pages as Becca spoke, gently caressing his pictures of Jackson.

"When we were at the beach party, Jackson said he was going to grab something and would be right back. I didn't know until afterward he had gone to get a soda, and you were there. He'd gotten such a knot in his stomach by the time he got to the table, he couldn't even talk to you, and it frustrated him to no end. He cursed himself as a coward for not speaking, feeling somehow unworthy of you because he couldn't even stand up for himself. He cried that night, upset because what he wanted he couldn't figure out a way to at least fight for. And it was that night I thought I'd won."

Knowing Jackson ached made Taylor's heart hurt. He wished the time they'd been apart had never happened.

"Jackson said he was glad things turned out like they did, Taylor," Becca said.

Taylor's breath hitched. Just for a moment, he thought she was reading his mind. "He believed it made him a stronger person, more mature. He realized had he gotten together with you in the beginning, his insecurities would have broken you up. He still held out hope he could be with you and be the kind of guy he thought you should have."

Taylor's eyes burned, and he was seriously close to crying. Jackson had always been the guy he wanted to have and now might never get the chance to be with.

"And that brings us to prom. We all know how that went," she said bleakly.

"Thank you, Becca. This really did help me."

"Taylor, can you ever forgive me?" she asked, hope obvious in her voice.

"I don't know if I could ever be friends with you, Becca," he answered honestly. "But, yeah, I can understand, and I can forgive. Jackson's heart is so big, I have no doubt he'd forgive you and probably want to be friends with you again at some point."

"Thank you, Taylor." She sniffed again. Her voice cracked when she continued. "That means a lot to me," she admitted. "Hey, have you talked to Jackson's father yet?"

Taylor realized he'd never even met Jackson's father. "No, I haven't. Do you think he'd want to meet me?"

"I guarantee it. Jackson talked about you to his father all the time. I know he'd want to get to know you too."

Becca gave him the number, said good night, and hung up. Taylor glanced at the clock. It was too late to try tonight, but tomorrow he'd definitely give Mr. Kern a call. He lay back on the bed, pulling the covers tightly around him. Some of the warmth from his conversation with Becca leeched out. Jackson had spoken to his father and told him about Taylor. Did that mean his father knew what happened? How Taylor had hurt his son? Would he want to see him, or would he tell him to stay away? Taylor didn't think he could bear it if he was forbidden to see Jackson.

AT THE end of the school day, Taylor called Jackson's father the minute he got home. He wasn't surprised to find him at the hospital. "Mr. Kern? Hi. I'm Taylor Andrews. I'm… a friend of Jackson."

"Well hello, Taylor Andrews. It's a pleasure to finally get to talk to you. Jackson told me a lot about you, and I'm glad I finally get a chance to hear your voice," he said enthusiastically.

"Thank you, sir. I was wondering if it would be okay for me to stop in and see you today? I was hoping to come down and see Jackson if you're going to be around."

"I'll be here for a while yet. You don't need to ask, just come on down. I really want to meet you."

Taylor's heart sped up. "I can be there in about twenty minutes if that works for you?"

"It sure does. I'll be here an hour or so yet. I'll see you soon."

As Taylor put away his phone, he noticed his palms were sweating. The thought of meeting Jackson's father caused his stomach to clench. He sighed deeply, let his parents know he was going to see Jackson, and drove to the hospital.

The antiseptic smell burned his nose as Taylor entered Jackson's room. A man Taylor assumed was Mr. Kern sat at the bedside, speaking softly. Taylor cleared his throat, and the man looked up.

"Mr. Kern? I'm—"

"You're Taylor. You're the boy my son loves." Mr. Kern dashed across the room, grasped Taylor's hand, and shook it enthusiastically. "It's a pleasure to meet you, son. Jackson's told me so much about you. I'm glad you came."

Taylor wasn't certain what to say. He hadn't been sure what Jackson had told his father about them, and he'd worried about saying too much. Knowing that Jackson had told him made it easier for Taylor to breathe. "I'm glad to meet you, too, sir."

"Lyle. My name is Lyle."

Taylor smiled. "Okay, Lyle." He paused. "How's Jackson doing?"

Lyle's face aged instantly. He turned to Jackson, padded back over to the chair, and slumped into it. "The doctors say he's going to be mostly okay. They were worried about nerve damage. He broke both legs and suffered a myocardial contusion, kind of like his heart was bruised. There's also some bruising on his brain too. They drained the blood around the heart and did surgery to repair blood vessels in his chest. They don't think there's going to be any major problems with that. The biggest problem is the bruising on his brain. They can't be sure what the long-term effects will be. They've kept him in a medically induced coma to try to give his body time to heal. It could be weeks before they know anything. He's young and healthy, though, so there's hope."

Taylor's heart sank. He wanted to comfort the man, but he had no idea what he could do or say to make it better. "I love your son, and I'm going to be there for him, no matter what, sir," he promised.

Lyle's face lit up. "Jackson told me you broke up with him, but he said he was going to give you time because he knew that it was going to be okay. He said he believed in you and that you'd make the right decision and come back to him."

Taylor's eyes began to fill with tears. He looked at Jackson longingly.

"Lyle, I think you need to know what happened between me and Jackson," Taylor said quietly. He recounted the whole story to Lyle. When he finished the story, he was emotionally drained at having to relive it yet again, but Jackson's dad needed to know the whole story.

Rising from his chair, Lyle gave a tight smile and hugged him. "You're a good man, Taylor. I truly appreciate what you did for my boy," he said. He released his hold and walked over to the bed.

"Come talk with him, son," Lyle encouraged, walking back over to Jackson's side. "I work nights and need to get going soon. I'd appreciate it if you would stay for a while."

Taylor nodded. Lyle squeezed Jackson's shoulder lightly and said, "He's here, son, just like you said he would be."

He patted Taylor on the back and left the room. Taylor took over the chair Lyle had been sitting in, placed his hand on top of Jackson's, and told him about his day.

PITCH

CHAPTER FIFTEEN
IT ALL COMES OUT

FOR the next several weeks, Taylor spent every free minute he had at the hospital. He and Lyle spoke often, Lyle telling him about Jackson's life before Milwaukee and Taylor filling him in on what he knew since.

"I know my boy wasn't happy moving all the time, Taylor," Lyle told him, "but I had to take the work where I could get it. I had seniority in the company and couldn't afford to take a different job, especially in the economy we have today. I figured Jackson resented me because he never had a real childhood," Lyle said glumly.

Taylor felt the need to reassure the man. "I don't believe he resented *you* at all, Lyle. I think he resented not being able to find his place in the world. It had to be hard for him, knowing everything he knew could be gone one day. I understand why he didn't want to make friends. It would kill me if I ever had to leave Benny behind."

"Yeah, Benny's a great guy. He's been a real pleasure to talk with. He would come in here, and just like that," Lyle said with a snap of his fingers, "he'd just make everything better."

Taylor laughed. "Yeah, he's like that. He just seems to have a gift."

"That the boy does. When he first started coming around, I thought he was interested in Jackson," Lyle admitted.

"Nah, Benny's straight."

Lyle looked at Taylor curiously. "You sure about that?"

"Yeah," Taylor said confidently. "He's just really in touch with who he is. He's always been a hugger."

Lyle arched an eyebrow. "He's your best friend. If anyone would know, it'd be you, right?" He smiled.

"When did Jackson tell you about us?" Taylor wondered.

"The boy wears his heart on his sleeve. I knew he was in love with someone, but it was a while before he told me. I kept telling him he shouldn't get his hopes up, especially since it seemed you weren't interested in him, but he's headstrong. He gets it in his mind, and he'll find a way to make it happen."

"I'm really glad he didn't give up on me, Lyle. He's the only person in my life who I've really wanted to share everything with. Benny gets me on most levels but not on all of them. Jackson told me he wants to understand it all." Taylor blushed.

"Yeah, he really does think you're special. When you broke up with him, he was crushed. He kept everything locked in so tight. He stayed home from school for a while because he wasn't sure he could face you. Then one day I pulled him over and sat him on the couch, and I made him tell me what was going on in his head. He looked at me for a long time, his bottom lip kept curling, and I could see his eyes watering. Then it all came out. He cried so hard, and all I could do was hold him. A few days later, he came to me and told me he'd decided you were going to be with him and no one could tell him otherwise. He said he wasn't going to let you go. He was going to force you to talk with him, to get it all out in the open, tell him what he'd done wrong and how he could fix it, but there was no way he was backing down without a fight. That night he went out for a run, and…."

Lyle looked down at Jackson, his eyes hard.

"Why did he do it, Taylor? Why did he hurt my boy?"

"He's sick, sir. He's really very sick."

Lyle walked over and threw his arms around Taylor, saying softly, "Thanks for being here with me, Taylor. Thanks for being with my boy. They stopped giving him the drugs that kept him asleep, but they don't know when he'll come around. I hope it's soon. I want him to talk with me again." He stepped back and brushed the back of his hand across his eyes. "I should probably get to work. Will I see you tomorrow?"

"Yes, sir. I'll be here, every day that it takes."

Lyle gave him a brief smile, pushed his fingers through Jackson's hair, and was gone. Taylor took the familiar spot next to the hospital bed and took Jackson's hand in his.

"I know you're still in there, Jackson. I need you to come back to me. Please? I thought I could be strong enough for both of us, but I can't. I'm barely holding it together. There are so many things I want to say to you, and I'm so afraid you'll look at me and want nothing more to do with... us. Please, I need you to come back," Taylor whispered.

He squeezed Jackson's fingers lightly, kissed the back of his hand, and drifted off.

The next thing he knew, Benny was shaking him awake. "Tay? Shouldn't sleep like that—it's going to get really uncomfortable."

Taylor rubbed his hand over his cheek, feeling the crease lines imprinted on his face where the blanket had pressed into his cheek. "Benny? What time is it?" Taylor asked, shaking his head to try and clear it.

"Visiting hours will be over pretty soon, but I wanted to stop in and check on both of you."

Taylor yawned and stretched, his spine popping as he did.

"I'm doing okay. No change with Jackson, though. I talked with his dad for a while today. He's a pretty cool guy. He likes you too."

"Well, that shows good taste on his part, then, doesn't it?"

Taylor chuckled at his friend. "He was right, Benny. Just by being there, you always seem to make everything better."

"Look, Taylor, I need to ask you something. Please don't be upset, okay?" Benny asked.

Taylor nodded.

"I got the paperwork today for Camp Care. It's only six weeks away, and I wanted to know what you were going to do."

Taylor glanced down at Jackson. "I can't leave him, Benny. Not again. Not until he knows I'm coming back to him."

Benny gave a lopsided grin. "That's what I figured. It works, too, because I don't know if they would have assigned you to work with me this year. I got a new partner."

Taylor frowned. Benny seemed so happy over the fact he wouldn't be going.

"Who? Is it someone I know?"

Benny's smile grew even bigger. "Yeah, definitely. Addy Dean is going to be working as a counselor this year, Tay. They're going to partner him with me because of my 'remarkable maturity'. Isn't that a laugh?"

Taylor regarded Benny with a new appreciation. "No, Benny. It's not. At all. I think they're right. You've always been one of the most levelheaded people I know. You don't just jump into stuff without having thought it through first. I think you and Addy together are a perfect fit."

Taylor chuckled as he watched his friend squirm under the praise.

"Thanks a lot. You don't know how much that means to me. If it hadn't been for you and your messed up infatuations, I never would have gone last year, and I would have missed out on meeting a remarkable person. So thanks for your sloppy study habits."

Taylor smacked his friend in the arm playfully. "Anything for you, Benny. Always."

Benny pulled Taylor in for a hug and froze. "Tay?"

Taylor looked at his friend, who was staring intently over his shoulder. Taylor turned around to see a pair of dark chocolate-brown eyes watching them. "Jackson? Oh God, Jackson!" he cried.

Benny ran from the room. Taylor hurried to the bed and pulled Jackson's hand to his chest. "Jackson? Can you hear me?"

Those beautiful eyes fixed on Taylor's face, but Jackson didn't say anything.

Nurses came rushing in, one saying, "Sorry, but you're going to have to step out while the doctors examine him," and quickly ushered him out of the room. Taylor called his parents, Becca, and Lyle to let them know Jackson had opened his eyes. Within the hour they were all at the hospital, waiting for word on how Jackson was doing.

"MR. KERN? I'm Dr. Williams. Jackson is awake but unable to communicate. He seems to know what's happening around him. He can focus on items. We're encouraged but still need to wait to see what, if any, the aftereffects are."

"What do you know so far, Dr. Williams?"

"As I said, Jackson seems to be able to focus, but as of yet he is unable to move. We're confident the paralysis is temporary, due to swelling around the spinal column resulting from the accident. We'll be taking him for an MRI and EMG tomorrow, looking to see if we can assess the damage to his body."

"Can we see him?" Lyle asked.

"Maybe one or two of you, but only for a few minutes. He still needs rest."

Lyle turned to Taylor. "Taylor? Will you come in with me?"

"Me?" Taylor squeaked.

Lyle nodded. "I want your face to be one of the first he sees. I need to give him a reason to come back."

Taylor walked with Lyle into Jackson's room. Lyle urged him to go ahead.

"Jackson?"

Jackson's eyes shifted over to Taylor.

"Hi. Thank you for opening your eyes for me. I've really missed you."

Jackson didn't seem to register what was being said to him, but his eyes stayed on Taylor's.

"I'm so sorry about what happened, Jackson. I didn't want to—" He stopped and looked over at Lyle, who smiled encouragingly.

"Tell him, son. Tell him what happened. Make him angry enough to fight, like he was that night."

Slowly, haltingly, Taylor told Jackson everything Kevin had done to him. Every demand Kevin had made. Every shred of dignity Kevin had stripped from him. He leaned over and whispered into Jackson's ear. "I still have nightmares. I haven't told anyone else, but I dream he took you from me, and I can't ever seem to find you, no matter how hard I look. I'll catch a glimpse and you'll be gone. I'll reach for you and you'll disappear. I wake up sweaty and scared. Then I remember he did try to take you away, and I was so afraid I'd never find you again."

Taylor brushed the hair from Jackson's eyes and saw the blaze of fury.

"I love you, Jackson. I have since the day I met you. I will until the day I die. When I wasn't with you, I had this huge hole in my heart and there was no way I could fill it. Kevin thought taking you from me would make me love him, but all it really did was crush me. I need you to come back to me, Jackson. I'm not too proud to beg for your love if that's what it would take."

Lyle stepped to the bed.

"Jax, you got quite a guy here. You were right. He's amazing, and I know you made the right choice. I could see it by the look in his eyes, hear it when he talked about you. This is the one you were meant to be with. So be with him, son. Come back for him. Let him give you the love you deserve."

Jackson's eyes closed as he drifted off to sleep, but Taylor swore there was a small smile on his lips. He turned to Lyle and saw him shaking, his face pale.

"Lyle? Are you okay?"

"You have to know how much I appreciate you," Lyle said softly, his voice choked with emotion. "I'm so glad you were here. I didn't want him to wake up alone. I can't tell you how grateful I am—" Lyle began sobbing harshly. Taylor rushed over and pulled Jackson's father into a tight hug, wincing as Lyle squeezed hard, burying his face into Taylor's neck, allowing Taylor to feel the heat of tears on his skin. "I honest to God thought he was gonna die and leave me alone. When his mom left, I was a wreck. I don't think I would have survived losing him."

Taylor quietly held on, rubbing Lyle's back, letting him release all the pent-up emotions.

THE EMG showed Jackson had sustained some nerve damage. While it was hoped he'd have a full recovery, it was possible he'd always have spasms or twitches in his muscles. They would likely be only moderate, the doctor said, but it would effectively end his chances at playing sports.

Taylor spent as much time as he could at the hospital. He sat with Jackson, watching him sleep, worrying that Jackson wouldn't forgive him, but he wasn't going to leave until Jackson told him to go. It took another week before Jackson woke up for more than a few minutes. He took Taylor's fingers and gave a gentle pull. Taylor smiled at him.

"Hey, welcome back, big guy. I missed seeing those pretty eyes of yours."

Jackson frowned, and Taylor moved his hand away.

"Look, Jackson, I can understand if you're angry with me. I didn't ever want to see you hurt, and I sure didn't want to be the cause of it. If you don't want to see me, I'll go, and I promise I won't come near you anymore. I just needed to make sure that you were okay. I'm sorry if I bothered you."

Taylor stood to leave, tears streaming down his cheeks. Jackson's hand moved out, and his fingers ran gently across Taylor's arm. He gripped Taylor's wrist and tugged lightly. Taylor wiped a sleeve across his face and peered into Jackson's eyes. Jackson kept a steady pressure on the wrist until Taylor came closer.

"Love Taylor," he croaked.

Taylor's face shone with happiness. He bent over and kissed Jackson softly on the lips, grinning against them when he heard the small, needy groan.

"Love Jackson," he whispered back.

Over the next week Jackson's voice grew stronger, and he was able to speak more clearly. After Lyle left one evening, Jackson asked Taylor to sit next to him. He was quiet for a few minutes as Taylor held his hand.

"What you did hurt me, you know," Jackson said softly.

"I know. It wasn't just you," Taylor admitted. "I upset a lot of people. I hurt Benny and my parents too. I was confused and didn't know what to do."

Jackson looked into Taylor's eyes and lowered his voice to a whisper. "I can't lose you again, Taylor. Not ever. I thought I'd die when you told me you didn't want to be with me. I can't go through that again."

"You won't have to. I didn't want to do it then. I couldn't imagine my life without you in it. I made a huge and stupid mistake. I promise no matter what else, I will always talk to you from now on. Deal?"

Jackson gave a small smile and pulled Taylor in for a long hug. "Sounds perfect to me," Jackson said, giving a slight sniffle.

JACKSON remained in the hospital for another three weeks. The staff introduced physical therapy slowly, helping muscles to strengthen and unworked limbs to become more limber. As the doctors had guessed, Jackson had residual nerve damage.

Taylor was sitting next to Jackson, reading to him, when Jackson's right arm began to twitch uncontrollably. Jackson stared at the limb for several minutes as the spasm continued. When the twitching finally subsided, Jackson looked up, cheeks turning red, and avoided making eye contact with him.

"Jackson, what's wrong?"

"I'm not… whole," he whispered sadly.

"What are you talking about? You're beautiful," Taylor countered, bending down to hug his boyfriend.

Jackson broke down, tears slide down his face silently. "I'm broken. I might never be normal again."

"Normal is overrated. I want you, you dope," he said, giving Jackson a bright smile. "Jackson, I want you the way you are, however that is. We can deal with everything else, but we'll do it together. You aren't going to get rid of me that easily."

"I'm not sure what my life is going to be like from now on. I can't play baseball. I don't know about student council. Are you sure you want to be stuck with me?"

"You're fishing for compliments, right? I don't care about baseball; I actually think it's a silly game. And student council? You were amazing. You might not be able to do all the physical stuff, but you have to know they're going to want you back. You also need to know that I'm going to be there with you."

Jackson looked into Taylor's eyes. "Love Taylor," he said with a grin.

"Love Jackson," Taylor replied, kissing him gently on the forehead.

A FEW days before Jackson was scheduled to be released from the hospital, Benny showed up and introduced Jackson to Addy.

"Hey, Jackson, you doing better?"

"God, yes. They finally took the casts off. I feel great."

"Cool, I'm glad to hear it. I got someone I want you to meet. This is Addy Dean."

"I'm really glad to meet you, Jackson. Benny's told me a lot about you. I'm glad you're doing okay," Addy said, extending a hand.

Jackson gripped Addy's hand, giving it a small shake. "It's good to meet you, too, Addy."

"We wanted to stop by on the way to Camp Care. Addy's going to be my co-counselor at summer camp this year."

Jackson's eyes flicked to Taylor.

"Aren't you going?"

"You're kidding, right? I'm not leaving you. My luck, you'll run off with some cute nurse or something."

"Why didn't you say something? This is important to you," Jackson huffed.

"I'm staying here to keep an eye on you. Do you have a problem with that?"

"No." Jackson laughed. "I think I can handle having you around."

Taylor sat back and watched the interaction between Jackson and Addy. He had told Jackson some of the things Addy had to overcome. He hoped seeing Addy now would help Jackson on the hard road ahead. He was really glad to see Addy too. Gone was the shy young man from last summer, replaced with a far more confident Adrian.

THEY visited for a while before Benny and Addy said their good-byes. Taylor crawled into the small hospital bed and put his arm around Jackson.

"I have to be honest, Taylor—when I thought about taking you to bed, this isn't quite what I had in mind," Jackson declared, waggling his eyebrows.

Taylor laughed and squeezed Jackson, pulling him in and wrapping around him. Jackson gave a soft moan.

"Am I hurting you?"

"Heck no. This feels so amazing. It's what I've wanted for a long time." Jackson sighed.

"I don't want to interrupt you, boys, but I need to check Jackson over," came an amused voice behind them. Turning, they found the nurse there, a wide grin on her face.

Taylor groaned and rolled off the edge of the bed and gave Jackson a kiss.

"You behave yourself. Remember what I said about running off with the cute nurse. I'm going to run down and grab a soda. I'll be back in a couple of minutes, okay?

"Just hurry back. These nurses are like vampires. You need to keep an eye on her to make sure she doesn't take more blood than I have to—OW! Taylor," he whined.

Taylor laughed and left the room, smiling over the fact that he could hear Jackson complaining all the way down the hall. He walked to the lounge area and pulled open the door. His jaw dropped at what he saw. There stood Benny Peters, his best friend since kindergarten, wrapped in the arms of Addy Dean, and they were kissing! Taylor watched for a few moments before he spoke up.

"Benny? Is there something you'd like to tell me?"

Benny looked up, his eyes glazed as he observed Taylor. His face was flushed, his cheeks red, as he simply stated, "No, Taylor, not right now." And he went back to kissing Addy.

Taylor smiled. It looked like Lyle was right after all. He was rather shocked but happy Benny finally had someone. He stepped out of the room and went back to Jackson, his smile growing wider. Oh, what a story he was going to have for him.

WILL PARKINSON believes that no matter what obstacles are thrown in the path of young love, it will always find a way to win in the end. He wants his characters to have their happily ever after, but that doesn't mean that it's going to come easily.

None of this would have happened if he had followed the advice he was given many years ago. "What are you wasting your time on that for? It's never going to amount to anything." He believed it for the longest time, abandoning characters he'd created in his childhood.

He picked up his very first m/m story by a writer named Eden Winters, who was an absolute joy when they corresponded. She asked him if he wrote and he told her the story. Eden explained to Will that the voices in his head would never go away and how he needed to let them out. With that thought in mind, Will put e-pen to e-paper once more. It was truly a liberating experience and one he has no intention of giving up again.

Website: http://www.willparkinson.com
Twitter: https://twitter.com/WillParkinsonau
Facebook: https://www.facebook.com/will.parkinson.520
E-mail: will@willparkinson.com

CHOICES

WAITING FOR FOREVER:
BOOK I

JAMIE MAYFIELD

http://www.harmonyinkpress.com

Also from HARMONY INK PRESS

DESTINY

WAITING FOR FOREVER:
BOOK II

JAMIE MAYFIELD

http://www.harmonyinkpress.com

Also from HARMONY INK PRESS

DETERMINATION

WAITING FOR FOREVER:
BOOK III

JAMIE MAYFIELD

http://www.harmonyinkpress.com

Also from H<small>ARMONY</small> I<small>NK</small> P<small>RESS</small>

Play Me, I'm Yours

Madison Parker

http://www.harmonyinkpress.com

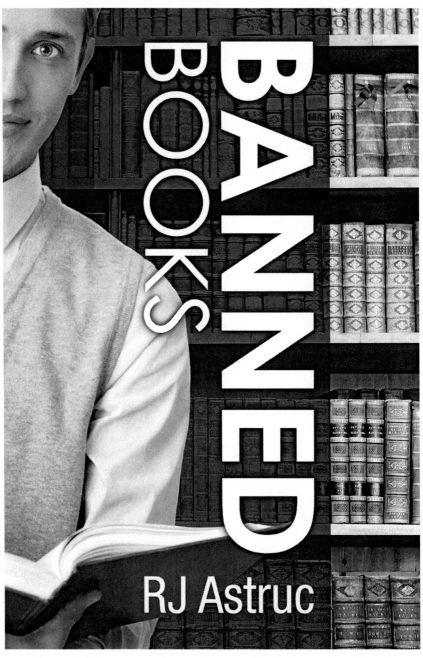

BANNED BOOKS

RJ Astruc

Also from HARMONY INK PRESS

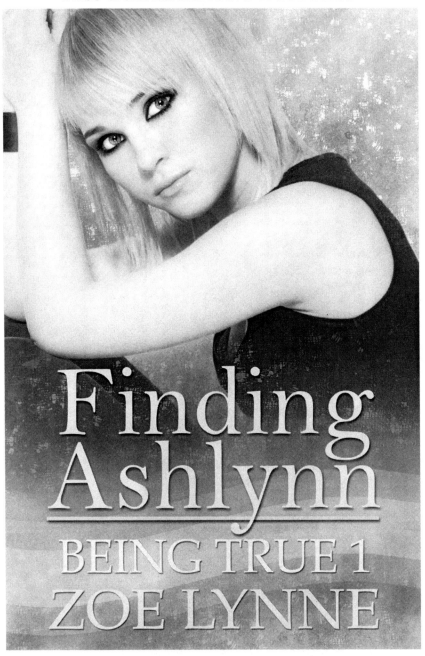

Finding
Ashlynn

BEING TRUE 1
ZOE LYNNE

Also from HARMONY INK PRESS

Everything
We Shut
Our Eyes To

Gene Gant

http://www.harmonyinkpress.com

Gene Gant

The
Battle
for
Jericho

http://www.harmonyinkpress.com

BULLIED

JEFF ERNO

http://www.harmonyinkpress.com

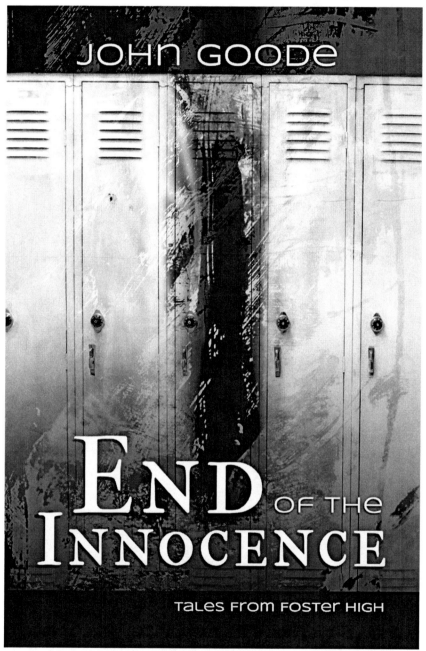

Harmony Ink

CPSIA information can be obtained at www.ICGtesting.com
Printed in the USA
BVOW03s2135110813

327869BV00005B/63/P

9 781627 980340